HEALING LOVE

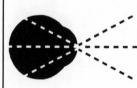

This Large Print Book carries the
Seal of Approval of N.A.V.H.

MONTANA SKIES #1

HEALING LOVE

THE LEGACY OF FAITH AND LOVE
CONTINUES

ANN BELL

THORNDIKE PRESS

An imprint of Thomson Gale, a part of The Thomson Corporation

THOMSON

GALE

Detroit • New York • San Francisco • New Haven, Conn. • Waterville, Maine • London

THOMSON
GALE
™

LIBRARY OF CONGRESS CATALOGING-IN-PUBLICATION DATA

Bell, Ann, 1945–
  Healing love : the legacy of faith and love / by Ann Bell.
    p. cm. — (Montana skies ; #1) (Thorndike Press large print candlelight)
  ISBN 0-7862-9136-2 (hardcover : alk. paper)
    1. Montana — Fiction. 2. Large type books. I. Title.
PS3602.E645425H43 2006
813'.6—dc22   2006030025

U.S. Hardcover:
ISBN 13: 978-0-7862-9136-6
ISBN 10: 0-7862-9136-2

Published in 2006 by arrangement with Barbour Publishing Inc.

Printed in the United States of America on permanent paper
10 9 8 7 6 5 4 3 2 1

Dedicated to the caring people of
Montana
who have devoted their lives to
comforting victims of violent crime.

CHAPTER 1

"Angie, can you hear me?" Serafina Cruz gasped as she knelt beside her friend's motionless body.

Angie didn't respond. A trickle of blood oozed from a cut on the side of her head.

Serafina's face blanched as she surveyed the darkened campus. In the distance a familiar figure emerged from the library. "Steve, hurry. Angie's hurt."

Steve Salas raced across the lawn of Guam Community College. "Oh, no. What happened? She looks terrible." He leaned closer and shook the injured woman's shoulder. "Angie, can you hear me?"

Angela Quinata moaned and turned her head. The look of terror in her eyes softened as she recognized her classmates. "Help me," she whispered. "I can't move." Steve turned and raced toward the phone in the entryway of the library.

Serafina brushed Angela's blood-soaked

dark hair away from her eyes. "Just relax. Steve's calling an ambulance. Everything'll be okay."

Angela closed her eyes, seemingly unaware of her friend kneeling beside her. Tears filled Serafina's eyes as she straightened Angela's rumpled skirt. "Please, God . . . Please help us. Angie's hurt, and I don't know what to do."

Serafina studied her friend's battered body. Her eyes settled on the scratches and bruises on Angie's legs. She pulled back in horror. "Please, God, don't let her have been raped. She's the most innocent girl I know. . . . Please help her."

Through the darkness, Serafina caught sight of Steve racing across the freshly mown lawn. "The ambulance is on its way," Steve shouted as he neared his classmates.

The minutes ticked by slowly as Serafina continued holding Angie's hand, while Steve paced nervously beside them. A warm trade breeze rustled through the palm trees. Their tense nerves jerked as a coconut hit the sidewalk and rolled onto the soggy grass. Angie's five-foot two-inch frame resembled a broken Barbie doll as she moaned and turned her head. She never responded to her friend's encouraging words.

Sirens pierced the tropical night air as red flashing lights reflected against the encircling palm trees. The ambulance screeched to a stop in the nearby parking lot, and three attendants jumped out. Two of them raced to the back, flung open the door of the ambulance, and pulled out a gurney, while the driver grabbed a large black kit.

Serafina released her classmate's hand as the Emergency Medical Team approached. The driver knelt beside the injured woman as Serafina stepped aside.

"What happened?"

"I don't know. I found her lying here covered with blood."

The driver wrapped a blood pressure tunic around Angela's arm and squeezed the ball as he stared at the gauge. He took a pen from his pocket and recorded his findings on a clipboard. "Both her pulse and blood pressure are a little low." He gently lifted her head. "It looks like she took a mighty powerful blow on the head, and she's lost a lot of blood."

The tall, graying attendant knelt beside the driver. "Do you see any other injuries?"

The driver shone his flashlight up and down her body. The light settled on Angie's trim legs. "Oh, no," he gasped. "I don't like the way her legs are bruised. We better admit her to the hospital as a possible rape victim."

The driver rose to his feet and moved the gurney as close to Angie as possible, while the other attendants positioned themselves at the victim's head and feet. They moved smoothly and methodically, so as not to cause additional pain to their patient. Angie moaned as the medical team lifted her gently to the stretcher. "Mama? Mama, where are you?"

Serafina's knees trembled as she again took her friend's hand. "Don't worry, Angie. Steve and I will follow the ambulance to the hospital. I'll contact your mother from the emergency room. Just relax . . . You're in good hands now."

Angie's eyes opened, and the corner of her mouth turned up slightly. Her mother's face flashed before her as she imagined her mother holding her in her arms as she did when she hurt herself as child. Gradually her eyes began to fade as her forehead creased once more. "Where's Mama?" she muttered, then closed her eyes.

Mitzi Quinata reread the letter she had just completed to a former colleague at Guam Christian Academy. Rarely had she made such a close friendship with a teacher from the mainland who stayed on Guam for only two years, just long enough to complete a teacher's contract, but Rebecca Sutherland Hatfield was different. She didn't carry the distant, aloof mannerism that many of the statesiders did. Rebecca appeared genuinely concerned for the Guamanians as people. She'd started several peer support groups for those in crisis and spent many hours before and after school counseling students.

Mitzi pictured her matronly friend as she was bidding her farewell at the Won Pat International Airport exactly one year before. Rebecca was aglow with the excitement of returning to Montana and her upcoming marriage. She had agreed to teach in Guam for two years after retiring from Rocky Bluff High School. Rebecca had walked to her plane anticipating a relaxing retirement, but her letters to Mitzi the last few months reflected a busy, productive life. Married life had been exhilarating for her. She described the beauty of the Montana mountains and the peacefulness of the small lake nearby. She talked about the friendliness of the people and their enjoyment of the outdoor sports available in that area.

I wish I could visit Rebecca in Montana, Mitzi smiled. *The way she describes it, Rocky Bluff is next to heaven on earth. Noth-*

ing could possibly be that perfect.

The ringing of the telephone interrupted Mitzi's thoughts. She laid her pen and paper on the kitchen table and hurried to the phone. "Hello."

"Hello, Mrs. Quinata?"

Wrinkles deepened on Mitzi's forehead as a knot built in her stomach. "Yes."

"Are you Angela's mother?"

"Yes, I am. Is something wrong?"

"I'm afraid so." Taking a deep breath, the young woman continued. "This is Serafina Cruz. I'm a classmate of Angie's. She was attacked on the GCC campus and taken to the hospital in an ambulance."

Mitzi's bronze face turned ashen. "What happened?"

"Steve Salas and I found her in the bushes between the administration building and the library. She was covered with blood. We called an ambulance and followed it to the hospital. Angie keeps asking for you."

"Tell her I'll be right there," Mitzi gasped as she flung the phone into its cradle.

She grabbed her purse and raced toward her car. A gentle rain soaked her flowered blouse and blended with the tears on her cheeks. *Please, God, help Angie. Don't let anything happen to her.*

The drive to Guam Memorial Hospital

normally would have taken Mitzi twenty minutes, but the traffic was light, and fifteen minutes after Serafina's phone call, Mitzi raced through the emergency room door.

"Mrs. Quinata?" Serafina said as the plump, graying woman stepped into the entryway.

Mitzi forced a smile and extended her hand. "You must be Serafina. Thank you for coming to the hospital with Angie. I'm so glad she has friends like you. How is she?"

"She's in X-ray right now." Serafina's words tumbled from her lips in rapid succession, while her voice became high and tense. "The nurse said that she's beginning to regain consciousness, and there are other positive signs. However, they can't be sure until all the tests are completed."

Mitzi's eyes roamed the corridors. "I've got to see her." She paced around the lobby looking for someone in charge. Her hands were clutched as the perspiration dripped from her forehead. "Where is everyone? There should be someone at the desk."

"There usually is," Steve replied, "but when they admitted Angie, they said they were short of staff tonight. I understand that several of the nurses are in Honolulu for a training session."

Mitzi continued to pace. "I can't understand how anything like this could happen. Angie's always so careful when she's out at night by herself."

Moments later, a nurse dressed in a white pants suit with blood stains on her smock hurried toward the concerned three. "Are you Angela Quinata's mother?"

"Yes, I'm Mitzi Quinata. How's Angie?"

"She received a severe blow to the head and has lost a lot of blood, but the X-rays didn't show any fracture to the skull. It took twenty-five stitches to close the wound. We'd like to keep her overnight for observation."

Mitzi studied the deep furrows on the nurse's face. "Do you think there'll be permanent damage?"

The nurse shrugged her shoulders. "The physical injuries will heal, but she's been sexually assaulted and is terribly upset. The emotional injuries are often the hardest to heal."

"Does anyone know who did it?"

"The police are on their way to interview Angie. I'd think it'd be best if you were present when they arrive. She needs a lot of moral support."

"I'll do everything I can," Mitzi choked, while her eyes filled with tears as she

14

noticed the reddish stains on the nurse's uniform. "Where is she?"

"Examining Room Four. Follow me."

Serefina waved good-bye as Mitzi obeyed the nurse. "I'll check with you tomorrow to see how she's doing."

Mitzi's knees trembled as she hurried down the hallway. She took a deep breath as the nurse pushed open the door to Examining Room Number Four. She stifled a gasp as she recognized her daughter. Angie was lying on the bed quietly sobbing. Both her eyes were blackened and swollen. The left side of her long black hair had been shaved and replaced by an enormous gauze bandage. "Hi, Darling," Mitzi whispered as she leaned over to kiss her daughter's forehead. "How are you?"

Angie clutched her mother's hand. "Mom, you're finally here."

"I came just as soon as I heard what happened."

Angie's sobs increased. "It was awful. I could withstand the beating, but a stranger stole what I was saving for my husband. I feel so dirty."

Mitzi bit her lip and tried to force a smile. "Angie, you're a brave girl. It's over now. Just relax and think about the bright future ahead of you . . . Graduation . . . a new career . . . romance."

"My future's over."

"No, Honey. You have your whole life before you. You'll feel better tomorrow. Saturday night is graduation, and you'll be receiving one of the highest honors in your class. Everyone is so proud of you."

"No, Mother. You don't understand. I can't attend my graduation. I won't be able to bear having people whispering about what happened."

"Of course no one will blame you. People will understand. You'll be surprised how compassionate people can be."

"That doesn't change the facts of what happened. My future's over. No man will ever want a spoiled woman, especially not the good ones like Jay."

Mitzi swallowed hard and wiped a tear from Angie's cheek. "Jay loves you. He'll accept you just the way you are."

"He deserves better. Besides, I can't let him see me now. Look how ugly I am. I'm covered with bruises, and part of my head is shaved."

"Angie, you'll be able to hide most of the bruises under makeup and get a wig to hide the bandages."

The pain of watching her bright, vivacious daughter in such depths of despair was

16

almost more than Mitzi could bear. Her words seemed trite compared to the magnitude of Angie's pain. "Your hair will grow back, and your bruises will heal. They're just surface injuries," she persisted as she wiped away the tears from Angie's cheek.

Angie's eyes became distant. She continued to cry for several minutes, while her mother stood helplessly beside her bed. "What did I do to deserve this? Why is God punishing me? Ever since I was a kid, I tried my hardest to please Him. Why did He let this happen?"

Mitzi studied her daughter's troubled face. "Darling, God isn't punishing you," she said as she squeezed her daughter's hand. "As long as there's evil in this world, bad things are going to happen. You just happened to be in the wrong place at the wrong time."

Angie shook her head. "I should have been more careful. I knew better than to stay so late, then walk across campus alone. God's punishing me for my stupidity."

"Angie, God doesn't work that way. Right now you're hurt and upset. After a night's rest, you'll feel better. As you close your eyes tonight, visualize yourself wrapped in God's loving arms."

"Mother, it's not all that easy. You don't

understand. You've never been raped."

Mitzi bit her lip. *I would lay down my life for her. Why doesn't she understand that I don't have to be raped to share her pain?*

Slowly, the examining room door opened, and the nurse entered, followed by two police officers.

"How are you doing, Angie?" the nurse asked as she approached the distraught patient.

Angie tried to gain her composure. "I don't think I'll ever be able to stop crying."

"You'll feel a little stronger tomorrow," the nurse assured her, then motioned to the two police officers. "I'd like you to meet Officers Irene Santos and Vincente Muñoz. They'd like to talk with you about what happened tonight."

Angie forced a smile as she surveyed the trim woman officer and her male partner standing rigid and businesslike. "Hello," she murmured.

"Hello, Angie," Officer Santos greeted as she reached for the young woman's hand and shook it gently. "Do you mind if we ask you a few questions?"

A lump built in Angie's throat. The thought of rehashing the events of the last few hours terrified her. "I don't remember much of what happened," she murmured.

"We'll try to make this as easy as possible. We know the trauma you've been through," Officer Santos said. Officer Muñoz carried two chairs from the waiting room and placed them on the left side of Angie's bed, while Mitzi remained seated on the right, unwilling to leave her daughter's side.

Officer Muñoz took a tape recorder from his pocket and placed it on the table beside the bed. "I hope you don't mind if we record this. We don't want to miss any details. We need all the help you can give us to find the person who hurt you before he hurts someone else."

Angie shrugged her shoulders with resignation.

"Angie, will you tell us exactly what happened tonight?" Officer Santos asked gently.

"I told you that I don't remember anything." Angie clutched her fists under the sheet. She just wanted everyone to leave her alone. Each question became more and more difficult.

"Let's take it step-by-step," Officer Santos replied gently. "I've worked with a number of women who were assaulted. The first time a victim talks about the attack is the hardest, and it occasionally takes awhile before they remember the details."

"I'll try my best," Angie whispered without

19

commitment.

"What was the last building you were in?"

"I took the final exam for my customer relations class in the main classroom building."

"What time was that?"

Angie hesitated. A look of puzzlement covered her face. Gradually a light of recognition appeared in her eyes. "I finished my test about eight-thirty, but I stayed after class to talk with the instructor. It must've been getting close to nine o'clock when I actually left the building."

"Did you see anyone else as you left?"

"No, the campus was deserted by then."

"Who was the instructor you met with?"

"Leon Paplos. He's an excellent teacher and is helping me get a job."

Angie did not notice Officer Muñoz stiffen at the name of the head of the cosmetology department at the community college, but Mitzi directed a puzzled glance at him which he ignored.

"Did Mr. Paplos leave at the same time you did?"

"No. He said he was going to work late and try to get most of the tests graded before he went home."

"As you crossed the campus did you see anyone else?" Officer Santos continued.

Angie's stomach tightened. "No one," she choked. "That's why I thought I'd cut across the lawn in front of the administration building to get to the parking lot."

"Then what happened?"

Angie remained silent for a couple moments, then began to sob uncontrollably. Mitzi leaned over the bed and cradled her daughter against her breast. "It's okay, Darling," she whispered, stroking her daughter's hair. "It's over now. You're safe with us."

Hearing Angie's hysterical cries, the nurse hurried back to the emergency room. She went to a cupboard in the corner of the room and unlocked the case. Meticulously, she filled a syringe as Mitzi continued to hold and comfort her daughter. "I think we'd better give her something to calm her. Being this upset is not good for her head injury."

Within seconds, the relaxing fluid entered Angie's bloodstream, and she lay back on her pillow and closed her eyes.

Mitzi tucked the blanket under her daughter's chin and returned to her chair beside the bed. "Poor dear, she's been through so much. I wish I could take her pain away."

"As much as you'd like to ease her pain, in the end, the victim is the only one who

21

can bring about healing," Officer Santos replied. "Healing comes in time, but the more that society victimizes the victim with its attitudes, the longer the healing takes."

"I hope Angie's strong religious background will help her conquer this, but so far it seems her training is more of a handicap than a help. Somehow she blames herself for what happened."

Officer Santos nodded with understanding. "Religious people often suffer the most emotional pain after a rape because they falsely blame themselves."

"What can I do to help her?" Mitzi begged as her eyes settled on her battered daughter.

"Only a proper understanding of the love of God can heal her pain," Officer Santos replied. "I wish I had an easy answer for you."

After the nurse disposed of the syringe, she turned to the police officers. "She's not going to be able to talk for awhile. Would you mind coming back tomorrow morning? We'll be moving her to a private room in a few minutes."

"We'll be back first thing in the morning. I hope she'll be able to talk then. We can't let the perpetrator get too far ahead of us."

Officer Muñoz picked up his tape recorder and placed it in his pocket. "We need to go by the campus and see if we can get any information. We'd like to have the attacker in custody as soon as possible."

Within minutes, two orderlies arrived and moved Angie to a private room on the third floor. Mitzi remained by her sleeping daughter's side until the wee hours of the morning. Finally, overwhelmed by mental and physical exhaustion, she scribbled her telephone number on a slip of paper and handed it to the ward nurse on her way out of the building. "Call me if Angie awakens and needs me. I better get some sleep tonight, or I won't be of much help to her tomorrow."

"We'll let you know if there's any change," the nurse assured her. "The best thing for you is to get some sleep. It's been quite an ordeal for both of you. We'll take good care of your daughter."

Mitzi left the hospital parking lot and turned onto Marine Drive. She scarcely recognized the well-traveled street. What was familiar to her in the daylight looked so different at night. In the daytime normal, middle class people went about their lives, earning a living, shopping, and visiting friends. Now the streets were full of prostitutes, pimps, and drug addicts. *I never knew this kind of lifestyle was present on Guam.*

I've always felt safe on our little island get-away.

As the lights of Agana disappeared into the background, Mitzi's mind drifted back to her sleeping daughter lying sedated in the island hospital. *I wonder what tomorrow will bring for her? Angie has to accept what has happened to her and go on with her life. She kept saying, "Jay will never want a spoiled woman." But I've found that Jay is the most understanding young man I've ever met. I'm sure he'll be the key to her recovery.*

As Mitzi turned onto the Cross Island Road, she pictured the tall, dark-haired airman from Andersen Air Force Base at the northern end of the island. Ever since Rebecca Sutherland introduced Angie to the young man from her hometown, Angie and Jay Harkness had been inseparable. Usually, Mitzi had ignored the large military population on the island, but somehow Jay was different. Like his former teacher and librarian, Jay took a special interest in the local people and their customs. He escorted Angie to as many of the fiestas and local celebrations as he could. However, it was obvious that Rocky Bluff was never far from his heart. As much as he was involved in island affairs, his heart was always in Montana. During the months that Angie had been dating Jay, Mitzi noticed the same interest in getting to know other peoples and cultures develop in her own daughter. *Would their love survive such a difference in backgrounds? Would this tragedy destroy or strengthen their relationship? Could Jay be able to restore her daughter's zest for living?*

When she got home, Mitzi stumbled toward her front door, unlocked it, and headed straight for the bedroom. Without removing her clothes, she fell across her bed. Every cell in her body was crying for sleep. For three hours she scarcely moved, but when the first rays of morning sun streamed through the east window, Mitzi bolted upright. *I have to talk to Jay before he goes to work. I don't want him to read about Angie's assault in the* Pacific Daily News.

Mitzi fumbled through the drawer under the phone and found her list of special phone numbers. She punched the numbers on the handset and waited for what seemed like an eternity.

"Hello," a sleepy voice greeted.

"Hello, is this Jay Harkness?"

"Yes, it is," the airman replied as he wiped the sleep from his eyes.

"This is Mitzi Quinata, Angie's mother." Mitzi took a deep breath as she tried to choose her words carefully. "I'm calling to let you know that Angie was admitted to the hospital last night."

Jay bolted upright in bed. "What happened?"

"Last night she was assaulted and raped as she was walking across the campus. She was knocked unconscious, and it took twenty-five stitches in her head to close the wound. They kept her in the hospital overnight for observation." Mitzi's voice trembled as she retold the details.

Jay was immediately on his feet. "Is she going to be all right?"

"I hope so," she sighed. "The nurse doesn't think there'll be any lasting physical damage, but Angie's extremely despondent. They had to give her a sedative. Hopefully, she'll be better today."

"That's terrible," Jay gasped. "I'll call my first sergeant right away and see if I can take the day off to be with her."

"Before you see her, I must warn you that she feels she's been ruined for life and that no man would ever want her again."

Jay sighed as he buried his face in his hands. A new tone of determination entered his voice. "She's not a spoiled woman to me. In the sixteen months that I've known her, she's become very precious to me. I'll just have to prove to her that God's love

26

and my love are stronger than her own fears and false guilt."

CHAPTER 2

An antiseptic smell permeated the corridors of Guam Island Hospital as Jay Harkness paused at the third-floor nurses' station. He was tall and imposing in his dress uniform. He had dreamed of being an airman since he was a child, and now he wore the United States Air Force blues with pride.

"May I help you?" the ward clerk asked as she removed her computer glasses and laid them on the counter beside her.

"Where may I find Angela Quinata?"

The clerk frowned as she surveyed the handsome, young airman. "She's in Room 314, but she won't be able to have visitors now. The police are with her, and it could be some time before they're finished. You can wait in the cafeteria if you'd like."

"Thanks, but if it's all right with you, I'd rather wait at the end of the hall. I want to be as close to her as possible."

"Suit yourself, but the waiting area on this

floor is rather limited." Jay turned the corner and strolled down the corridor. He paused in front of Room 314. The door was closed. He took a deep breath. The girl he loved was behind that door, yet he could not go in. Glancing around he noticed a sofa under the window at the end of the hall. Dejectedly he slumped onto the lumpy cushions. *This is the time Angie needs me the most, and I'm not able to be with her. I bet she's scared to death.*

Jay stared at the hands of the hall clock for what seemed like hours. Only the second hand appeared to move. While growing up, he had spent a great deal of time visiting in hospitals during his grandparents' long illnesses, but that was nothing compared to the desperation he felt waiting to see his best friend and sweetheart. The young airman surveyed his drab surroundings. Everything was scrubbed clean, but the paint on the walls was faded, and the fixtures were antique compared to the modern community hospital in Rocky Bluff. *If only I could take Angie back to Montana where she'd get personalized care with the latest technology and professionals.*

The large hand on the hall clock inched its way to the bottom of the case. Jay watched the hospital personnel go about their routine tasks. The hustle and bustle of Montana hospitals was strangely missing. Activity was relaxed and slow, yet the work seemed to get done quietly and efficiently. At long last, two police officers emerged from Room 314 and closed the door gently behind them.

"She'll probably never recover from this," the woman officer whispered to her partner. "In all my years of rape investigation, I've never dealt with a victim who felt it was so important to save herself for her future husband. With her self-imposed guilt I wonder if she'll ever marry."

The male policeman shook his head. "I thought that attitude went out with the sexual revolution of the sixties."

"With all the sexually transmitted diseases going around today, I wish more young people had Angie's values. It would make our job a lot easier."

As soon as the officers turned the corner at the nurses' station, Jay knocked softly on the door.

"Come in." It was Mitzi's voice.

Jay gasped as he scarcely recognized Angie who was sobbing into her pillow. Mitzi was sitting on the side of her daughter's bed, rubbing her back gently.

"Hello, Jay. I'm glad you could come. Did

you have to wait long?" Mitzi queried.

"Too long," Jay replied as he hurried to Angie's bedside. "I've been here about a half hour." He put his hand on Angie's shoulder and spoke softly. "Angie, how are you doing?"

She rolled over and shook her head vigorously. "Talking with the police was absolutely awful," she cried. "They expected me to remember every detail that happened. . . . But it was dark and I couldn't see anything. . . . I tried to fight, but the man was too strong. Then he hit me over the head."

"Whoever did this to you should be behind bars," Jay snarled, then tried to soften his approach as Angie grimaced. "It sounds like the police don't have a good description to go on."

"I'm afraid not. There was something distinctive about him, but I can't put my finger on it," she sighed. "Maybe someday it'll come to me. But now I don't want to remember what happened. . . . It's too ugly."

Jay stroked her forehead. "It's over, Sweetheart. We can go on with our lives and forget all this. . . . When will you be able to go home?"

Angie wiped the tears from her eyes and set her jaw firmly in place. "I'll never be able to forget this." She pounded her fist into the mattress, then paused. She took a deep breath and tried to force a smile. "The doctor said I can go home by noon . . . which is none too soon for me. I just want to get to my own apartment . . . away from this maddening world."

"Hospitals have never been my favorite place, either," Jay agreed sympathetically. "I'll drive you home when you're released. I've taken the entire day off work so I'll be able to stay with you for awhile."

"Jay, I'd appreciate you staying with Angie for a few hours. I don't want her to be alone in her condition," Mitzi whispered, unable to mask her fatigue. "I'd rather have her come home with me for a few days, but she insists on being in her own apartment. Knowing she's in good hands, I can go home and rest without worrying. I'll call you later in the evening."

Angie's eyes danced. "You don't have to fuss over me," she protested. "I'm able to take care of myself. I don't need to be pampered."

Jay took her hand and pressed it to his lips. "Angie, we love you and want to help you."

Tears again gathered in Angie's eyes as she pulled her hand away from his. "Jay, our relationship is over. I vowed I would keep myself pure for my future husband, and now I'm ruined." She fumbled with the friendship ring on her finger and placed it in Jay's palm. "Take your ring back. I'm never going to have anything to do with men again."

Mitzi watched as the pain built in Jay's eyes. They exchanged panicky glances. Each hoped the other had the magic words to calm her, but neither did. Jay clutched Angie's hand next to his cheek. "Sweetheart, you're still the same beautiful woman you were yesterday at this time. Your body and spirit may have been wounded, but God's in the healing business. I'll keep this ring in my pocket, and when you're feeling better, I'll be honored to place it back on your finger. I still love you, and God still loves you."

"That may be so, but I don't feel God's love . . . I feel He's abandoned me. Why did He let this happen?" Angie surveyed Jay's worried face as she continued to bombard him. "Can you answer my question? Why did this have to happen to me?"

"Angie, don't torture yourself with all these questions. You were simply in the wrong place at the wrong time," Jay said, holding her hand as he sat on the edge of the bed. "As long as there's evil in the world, bad things are going to happen to good people. But God still loves you regardless of what happens. He gives us strength to get through the rough times."

Angie shrugged her shoulders in disbelief. "That's what Mom said," she retorted, "but when I look at my bruised body and remember what I lost last night, how can I possibly feel God's love?"

"Fortunately, God's love is not based on our feelings. It's present even when we're least aware of it. Your Christian friends will support and uphold you with love and prayers until you can feel God's love again."

"I wish I could believe you," Angie sighed, "but I'll never be the same again."

"Of course you won't be the same. In the end you'll be a much stronger person, able to help others going through similar situations."

The door creaked open. A doctor and a floor nurse entered the room. Angie immediately pasted a phony smile on her face.

"How are you doing today?" Dr. Cruz asked brightly. "Are you ready to go home?"

Angie smiled. "You better believe it," she replied, trying to act equally as bright. However, her words could not mask her inner turmoil. *If the doctor knew how I really am, he'd never let me out of here.*

The doctor glanced at Jay and Mitzi, then turned back to his patient. "Angie, if your guests will step outside the room, I'll do a quick examination. If everything checks out, you can be on your way."

"I can hardly wait," she said, sitting upright in her hospital bed.

"I wish I could leave as well," the doctor chuckled. "It's a beautiful day outside. The sun's shining, and there's a slight trade breeze."

As Dr. Cruz took out his stethoscope, Mitzi and Jay walked into the hallway. The worried mother smiled at the young airman as they approached the sofa at the end of the corridor. "I'm glad you came. I could talk and talk but never get Angie to accept the fact that she's still the same person she was yesterday. You're the best one to get through to her."

Jay shook his head and sighed. "I'm not doing a very good job of it right now."

"You're doing a lot better than I am. Angie needs your love now more than ever."

Jay shook his head and wrung his hands. "I feel so helpless," he confessed as he watched a ship sail from nearby Apra Harbor. *If only my family were here to help me. I need more wisdom now than I ever have in my life,* he thought as he pictured his mother's and grandmother's faces.

He turned back to Mitzi. "With God's strength I'll do my best to help her," he sighed. "I never realized how much I loved her until I saw her there, bruised and hurting. She's a woman worth waiting for."

Angie's mother nodded knowingly. "I feel equally helpless. I wish I could suffer this pain in her place," she sighed. "Watching her suffer is breaking my heart."

The pair sat in silence for several minutes. Words could not express their grief. Finally Mitzi spoke. "After I take a nap, I'm going to get a letter off to Rebecca Hatfield asking her to pray. While she was librarian at my school, she seemed to have a direct pipeline to heaven. I don't know anything about Rocky Bluff, Montana, but I've met two dynamic Christian people from there."

Jay's face flushed as a slight grin covered his lips. "That's nothing; you should meet my grandmother," he replied with marked pride. "Her body may be wearing out, but she's a tremendous prayer warrior. She may not be able to get out as much as she used to, but we all know we have Grandma's prayers supporting us. As soon as I can, I'm going to call Mother and ask her to call Grandma. When Grandma prays, things happen."

Mitzi stared out the window at the parking lot lined with palm trees. *So much has happened in the last twenty-four hours. Will we ever be able to restore our lives to normal again?* They sat in silence as the clock ticked softly beside them. Mitzi became pensive. "I wish I had your grandma's kind of faith, but I become too impatient when my prayers aren't answered right away. . . . To be honest, this is the first time my faith has really been put to the test. Sure, little things have happened, but never anything like this."

"Grandma's been through a lot in her life, and instead of giving up and becoming bitter, she drew closer to the Lord. Everyone in town looks up to her. They even named the new wing of the high school after her."

"What an inspiration. I'd like to go to Rocky Bluff someday, if she's an example of the kind of people who live there. Guam has become such a melting pot of nationalities that we've lost our own identity. No one seems to care much about anyone else anymore. It's not what it used to be."

"Don't get the wrong idea. Rocky Bluff isn't heaven on earth, regardless of what Rebecca led you to believe," Jay tried to explain. "We've more than our share of problems and crime, but we always hang together during a crisis."

Now it was Jay's turn to become pensive. He pictured the small lake just outside of town with the Rocky Mountains providing a protective tower. He remembered the Easter sunrise service held on the banks of its glistening waters. He thought of his favorite Scripture, *"I lift up my eyes to the hills — where does my help come from? My help comes from the Lord, the Maker of heaven and earth."* He ran his hands across the knees of his uniform and stared down the hallway. "In a way Rebecca is right. Rocky Bluff is a special place. When I graduated from high school, I couldn't wait to get away from there, but regardless of how much I love Guam now, I'm counting the months until I can get back."

Mitzi nodded and placed her hand on the airman's shoulder. "That's so common around the world. Many of our graduating seniors hurry to the mainland, but one by one they return. There's something in each of us which yearns for the place of our upbringing. Some people can move home again, but others only return in their hearts."

Just then the door of Room 314 opened. The nurse turned toward the nurses' station, while the doctor headed toward the anxious pair waiting on the sofa.

Jay and Mitzi rose as he approached. "Angie's doing fine. With a little rest and a lot of tender loving care, she'll be back to normal in a couple days. However, she needs to see me in my office in five days to have the stitches taken out of her head and to do more tests."

Mitzi extended her hand to the doctor. "Doctor, thanks for all you've done. I feel that Angie has the best care available anywhere."

"Thank you, Mrs. Quinata. You have a lovely daughter," he replied as he shook her hand. "One other thing," he continued cautiously. "Keep an eye on her mental state. Her faked cheerfulness doesn't fool anyone. She's in a deep state of depression. Hopefully, it will lift in a few days; otherwise I'd suggest seeking outside counseling."

"We'll keep a close eye on her. She has a lot of friends and family to help her through this."

"Tender loving care and time are the greatest healers in the world," the doctor said as he turned to leave.

Mitzi and Jay returned to Angie's room where she was sitting on the edge of the bed trying to comb what little hair she had left.

"Are you ready to go home?" Jay teased.

Angie grinned. "The sooner the better."

"Good. I'll bring the car to the front entrance while your mother helps you dress. Just remember you're going to be stepping into a different and brighter world. You can now be categorized as a survivor. You can have the confidence that with God's help you are able to conquer anything."

"I may be a survivor, but I don't have the confidence to face the outside world," Angie retorted. Jay leaned over and kissed her gently on her lips, muffling her protests.

As Jay left the room, a sense of determination overwhelmed him. He would do his best not to let Angie dwell on the negative, but it was going to be difficult to put any type of positive spin on Angie's tragedy.

Jay parked his car near the emergency room door and met Angie and Mitzi at the doorway. Mitzi hugged her daughter, then said good-bye to Jay. She walked to her car in the distant parking lot, while Jay helped Angie to his car parked in the loading zone.

As they entered the hospital courtyard, Angie blinked against the tropical sun. *What right does the sun have to keep shining when my world has fallen apart? I'd feel much better if a torrential rain were falling.*

Sensing her uneasiness, Jay put his arm around her shoulder. "Are you all right?"

Angie shrugged her shoulders. "I wish I had a hat," she said as Jay opened the car door for her. "I don't want anyone to see my shaved head and bandages."

"After you're settled into your apartment, I'll run to the mall for you," Jay promised. "Let me know if there's anything else you'll need. My time is your time for the rest of the day."

Angie heaved a sigh of frustration. "I'm embarrassed to say this, but I'll need a pair of heavy-duty sunglasses. I don't want anyone to see my black eyes."

Jay slid behind the wheel, fastened his seat belt, and started the engine. "No problem at all," he assured her. "But first let's stop for some hamburgers. I'm famished, aren't you?"

"Not really, but I guess it is getting close to noon."

Angie sat rigidly in her seat as Jay drove the familiar streets of Agana. *I wonder if the driver of that car is the one?* she thought every time they passed a car driven by a male. *This is ridiculous,* she scolded herself. *I've got to get hold of myself.* Angie tried to focus on her immediate surroundings as Jay neared their favorite fast-food restaurant.

They ordered drinks, fries, and cheeseburgers at the drive-thru window. The aroma of the French fries activated Angie's sense of hunger. She unwrapped the sack and popped a couple of fries in her mouth as Jay drove toward her apartment. She could hardly wait for the comforts of her simple home. Arriving at Angie's complex, Jay parked in the vacant slot beside Angie's red Honda and helped her inside.

Angie stopped at her mailbox in the front of the building. "I suppose I better check my mail," she said as she fumbled in her purse for her keys. "I usually don't get anything but advertisements, but I keep hoping that today will be my lucky day, and I'll receive good news through the mail. . . . Yesterday definitely was not a lucky day."

She unlocked her box and fumbled through the "Current Occupant" brochures. A white business envelope was last in the pile. With trembling hands she tore it open as Jay waited silently beside her. She silently read the small print, then let out a scream of delight and threw her arms around Jay.

"I got it. I got it!"

"Got what?"

"I got the job at Coiffure and Manicure Beauty Salon in the Agana Mall. That's the best salon on the island. They want me to start a week from Monday."

"Fantastic," Jay exclaimed as he embraced

her. They were both momentarily caught up in the joy of the news. "Let's go upstairs and eat these cheeseburgers to celebrate."

As they entered Angie's modest, one-bedroom apartment, Angie's mood shifted dramatically. "I can't start work in ten days. Look at me. My hair won't be grown out, and I'm covered with bruises."

"Your bruises should be pretty well healed in a week," Jay reminded her. "With your knowledge of makeup, I'm sure you'll be able to mask the remaining discoloration. Tell you what, when the stitches come out, I'll buy you a nice blond wig," he teased.

Angie giggled through her frustrations. "Now wouldn't I look great as a blond with my dark complexion and dark eyes?"

"You'd look good even if you were bald. Now let's eat our food before it gets cold," Jay quipped.

Jay and Angie spread their food bags around the kitchen table. Momentarily Angie forgot the trauma of the night before. "Coiffure and Manicure is the most prestigious salon on the island. Everyone tries to be hired by them, but they only take the very best. That's why I didn't expect to be selected."

"You are the best," Jay reminded her. "You're graduating with honors."

Angie took another bite from her hamburger. "I think my instructor, Leon Paplos, had something to do with me getting the job. He's a good friend of the owner."

"What else do you know about the salon?"

Angie's eyes reflected a momentary twinkle of her old self. "I've heard the owner is one of the most eligible bachelors on the island."

"Are you saying I'm going to have competition?" Jay teased.

Angie grinned, then became suddenly serious. "Of course not. He's definitely not my type. . . . I've heard a lot of rumors about his nightlife, but I'm sure it's just idle gossip."

Jay took Angie's hands in his and gazed into her eyes. "I just want you to know how much I love you, and I want to share the rest of my life with you."

"Jay, don't. . . . Please . . . I'm no longer the innocent, pure young woman that you deserve."

"Angie, how can I convince you that no matter whatever happened to your body, your soul and spirit are still pure."

Tears welled up in her eyes as she bit her lip to choke back sobs. "If only I could go back to what I was before I left class last night."

"Darling, how many times must I remind you that you are the same person I fell in love with and want to marry?"

Jay painfully watched Angie shrug her shoulders and take another sip of her Coke. *What am I doing wrong in trying to convince her of my love? Does my love appear that shallow?*

After finishing her lunch, Angie rose from the table and yawned. "Jay, I hate to leave you with nothing to do, but I've got to take a nap. I'm so tired I can hardly keep my eyes open."

"That's the best thing for you. I'll be here if you need anything. In fact I may take a quick nap on the sofa myself."

Angie disappeared into her bedroom, while Jay thumbed through the travel magazines on her coffee table. After Angie had been sleeping for half an hour, Jay reached into his wallet and took out his telephone calling card. He took the phone from its cradle and punched in a series of familiar numbers. The clicks of connections being made amazed him as he envisioned the telephone signal bouncing up to the satellite and finally coming to rest in his parents' home in Montana.

"Hello," a sleepy voice mumbled.

"Hello, Mom. Did I wake you?"

"I should be getting up anyway," Nancy Harkness yawned. "I've got a lot to get done today. How are you?"

"I'm fine, but it's not me I'm concerned about. I'm calling to ask for prayers for Angie Quinata."

Nancy sat up straight in bed. "What happened?" she asked as she swung her legs over the side of the bed.

"She was attacked and raped while she was walking across campus last night." Jay took a deep breath and glanced toward the closed bedroom door behind which Angie was sleeping. "She now has twenty-five stitches in her head and is an emotional wreck. She thinks she's ruined for life and that no man will ever want her, especially me."

"How awful," Nancy gasped. "We'll be sure and remember both of you. I'll call your grandmother right away and ask her to pray as well."

"I'd appreciate that. Angie needs all the prayer support she can get. Would you also call Rebecca Hatfield, as well? If it wasn't for her, I never would have met Angie."

"I'm going to be seeing Rebecca this afternoon at the community bazaar. I'll tell her about Angie," the attractive, middle-aged woman promised as she reached for her fleece robe. "She's another one who's become a real prayer warrior."

"Thanks, Mom. I appreciate all your help. You and Grandma have always been my greatest sources of encouragement." Jay's voice nearly broke as he ended the conversation. "I love you all, and I miss everyone in Rocky Bluff. I can hardly wait to get back."

"I love you too, Son. Good-bye for now. We'll all be praying for both Angie and you."

"Good-bye, Mom."

That afternoon as Nancy Harkness was admiring a collection of embroidered wall hangings, she spotted Rebecca Hatfield browsing through a nearby booth. "Rebecca, how are you?" she greeted. "I haven't seen you in ages."

"I've been extremely busy lately. Working four hours a day at the florist's, plus my volunteer work at the historical library, I haven't been out and about much," Rebecca replied. "We have a lot of catching up to do. Let's go over to the food booth, and I'll treat you to a piece of pie and a cup of coffee."

"Sounds good. However, I was planning to invite you. I have something I need to talk with you about."

The two longtime friends headed toward the northwest corner of the community center where the Rocky Bluff Garden Club was holding a food fair. After selecting their favorite piece of pie and pouring themselves a cup of coffee, Nancy and Rebecca found an empty table in the back of the booth.

"You look upset. What's wrong?" Rebecca asked.

Nancy shook her head. "I didn't know it was that obvious," she replied softly, "but I'm worried about Jay and his friend, Angie Quinata."

"What happened?"

"Jay called this morning and asked us to pray for Angie. He said she was raped last night as she was leaving class. He said it took twenty-five stitches to close a wound in her head, but he was more concerned about her mental state."

"Poor Angie. She's such a sweet girl. This could traumatize her for life. I know what she's going through. Something similar happened to me when I was her age."

Nancy could not hide her shock. "I'm sorry," she said as she reached for Rebecca's hand. "You've never told me this before. You've always seemed so well-adjusted."

Rebecca lowered her eyes. "It's something I don't like to talk about, but if I can use my pain to help bring healing for someone

48

else, it's well worth speaking out. I wish I could bring Angie here to spend several weeks with me. I'd try to love her out of her misery."

"That'd be nice," Nancy agreed, "but the chances of Angie ever coming to Montana are almost nil. Jay says their relationship hangs in the balance unless she comes to grips with what happened. He seemed terribly discouraged."

"Nothing's impossible. Prayer and love were able to restore my life, and I'm confident they'll also restore Angie's."

CHAPTER 3

Angie stood in front of the full-length mirror and adjusted her new shoulder-length wig. She scowled as she wrapped a strand of hair behind her ear.

"Angie, you look terrific," Jay encouraged. "You'll be a hit at your graduation tonight."

"The wig might look okay, but it hurts," she fumed. "I don't think I'll be able to wear it until the stitches come out. Even if I wanted to, I won't be able to go tonight."

Jay shook his head in frustration. Nothing he said seemed to make any difference. "I wish you weren't so self-conscious about your appearance. People will understand you've been through a lot in the last few days."

"But I don't want their sympathy. I don't want anyone to say, 'Oh, she's the poor thing who's been damaged for life.' "

Jay pulled her close. Angie's lips trembled as she buried her face against his shirt.

"You're not damaged goods. You're beautiful. I'd be proud to escort you to your graduation or anyplace else. Do you have a scarf you could wear?"

"Let me check." Angie went to her dresser and rummaged through the bottom drawer. "I do have this black-and-gold scarf. Maybe I can tie it so it looks like a fashion statement and not just something to hide my shaved head."

Angie returned to her mirror and folded her scarf in a modified triangle. With a few added folds she was able to make a turban. She pulled out a few locks of hair around her face.

Jay stepped back and cocked his head. "Hmm. Not bad. You're definitely making a fashion statement with that. You'll be the hit of the ceremony."

"I wish I could put my head in a bag, but I guess this'll be okay," Angie stated dejectedly. "At least I won't be letting everyone down by not attending."

"Great. Let's call your mother and see if she wants to join us for dinner at the Garden Plaza. After the ceremony we can all go to the reception at the Commons."

Angie remained unconvinced but gave in to Jay's persistence. She was split between her old rational self and her current mental turmoil. *Will anyone ever understand what I'm going through?*

Angie shrugged her shoulders. "Yeah, I guess," she sighed. "I've already paid the rent for my cap and gown." She reached for the phone. Her fingers touched the familiar sequence of numbers without hesitation.

"Hello."

"Hello, Mom. How are you?"

"I had a good night's rest, and I'm doing fine. More importantly, how are you?"

"I guess I'm okay," Angie replied, unable to hide her frustrations, "but I won't be able to wear my new wig. It looks all right, but it hurts where the stitches are."

"Would you like me to bring some of my scarves along? Maybe one of them will be the right size and color."

"Thanks for the offer, Mom, but I think I'll wear my black-and-gold one. It's not the best, but it's passable," Angie replied. She searched for encouragement from Jay. He grinned and winked at her. The tension faded slightly from Angie's face. "Mom, I was wondering if you'd like to join Jay and me for dinner at the Plaza Gardens? Jay insists on making a big celebration out of my graduation."

"Angie, don't sound so dejected. This is a

time for celebration," Mitzi persisted gently. "I can hardly wait. Would you like me to drive?"

"No, Jay's going to drive. Meet us here at five-fifteen, and we'll go together."

Early that evening the threesome gathered in a corner booth at the finest restaurant on the island. Each ordered Steak Albert, the entree which had made Plaza Gardens famous in Guam. When the steaks arrived, Jay and Mitzi were overcome by the delicious aroma; they ate heartily, while Angie merely picked at her food. To her the entree held no flavor.

"Honey, what's wrong? You've hardly touched your dinner," Mitzi said as she took another sip of her coffee.

Angie stared blankly out the window at the sun setting behind the distant beach. "Oh, nothing. I'm just not hungry."

"Are you nervous about the ceremony?"

"The ceremony's no big deal," Angie shrugged. "I haven't missed a college graduation ceremony in three years. I've watched all my friends graduate." She hesitated and took a deep breath. "It's just that I don't want to go back to the campus."

Jay put his arm around Angie's shoulder and pulled her closer to him. "You won't be alone. Your mother and I will be in the audience, and you'll be surrounded by your friends."

"It's not that . . . It's . . . it's the memories."

Mitzi's eyes studied her daughter's black-and-gold turban and the heavy makeup that hid her fading bruises. "Angie, you'll make new memories tonight. You'll walk across that stage the third-highest-ranking student in your class. That's a memory you'll cherish forever."

Angie's lip began to tremble. "Do you think anyone will notice the award? They'll all look at the scarf and say, 'She's the poor girl who was raped leaving class the other night.' "

Jay continued to hold her next to himself. "Angie, God will give you strength to face your fears. If you hide from them now, they'll keep getting bigger and bigger. Do your best to confront them, please. Your mother and I will be there to cheer you on."

A waitress in a black-and-white uniform stopped at their table and inquired about the food. After receiving two affirmative nods, she left the bill on the corner of the table and slipped away, conscious of the fact that something extremely personal was happening and her customers needed their privacy.

The trio finished eating in relative silence, each lost in their own thoughts of helplessness. Jay reached for the bill, and the three walked silently to the front. He handed the hostess his credit card, waited for the receipt, and signed his name. Their celebration dinner had been a dinner of dismal formality and unresolved pain.

Tension filled the car as the three rode to the campus of Guam Community College. Jay and Mitzi exhausted every combination of words trying to console Angie who sat in sheer terror, but to no avail. Angie sat stiffly in the front seat beside Jay.

Upon arriving at the campus, Jay parked his car in the lot behind the baseball field. He opened the car door for Angie and her mother, then reached into the backseat for the box containing Angie's graduation gown and mortar board. He tucked the box under his left arm and offered his right arm to Angie. He could feel her arm trembling as it encircled his. "You're doing great," he whispered. "You'll be able to face your fears and conquer them."

"I'll do my best, but I can't guarantee anything." Angie sighed. "I feel so weak and inadequate."

Mitzi strolled beside the young couple, caught up in the excitement of the evening she had long been anticipating. "Look at the moon," she commented, unaware of the continued tension beside her. "I've never seen it this full and bright before. The campus is so peaceful tonight with the breeze rustling through the palm trees. It's a perfect night for an outdoor ceremony."

Jay and Angie did not respond to Mitzi's words but slowly walked toward the stadium where the graduates were assembling. Angie clutched his arm tighter with each step. As they neared the library, Angie's trembling became more apparent. She bravely took a deep breath, but when she saw the bushes where she had been raped, Angie screamed, "Take me home. Take me home."

"Angie, this is your big night," Mitzi insisted. "You've got to go on."

"I can't. I can't do it. Jay, please take me home."

Angie collapsed against Jay's chest. He wrapped his arm around her to support her weight. She stood there trembling and sobbing several minutes. Mitzi tried to encourage her to go on, but to no avail. Finally, Jay took Angie's face in his hands. "Everything's going to be all right. I'll take you home."

The sidewalk was now crowded with cheerful graduates and their families heading toward the stadium as the trio wove their way back to the parking lot. "Isn't that Angela Quinata?" a girl whispered to her friend.

"Yeah, I think so," her friend whispered back. "She looks terrible."

Angie's knees weakened under her, and she collapsed onto the sidewalk. Jay scooped her into his arms and carried her to his car. Mitzi opened the door for him as he laid the stricken graduate gently on the backseat. Mitzi squeezed into a corner of the seat beside her daughter, while Jay opened the front door and started the car.

Jay headed toward Angie's apartment. Her sobs subsided as they neared her familiar street. Parking his car in front of the complex, Jay opened the back door so Mitzi could alight. He took Angie's hand in his. "Do you think you'll be able to walk?"

"As long as I have your arm to hold onto, I'll be fine," she whispered as she slid from the backseat and wrapped her arm in his. "I'm sorry I'm such a bother and disappointment. I know how much you and Mother wanted to see me graduate."

"We're proud of you for making such a brave effort. Anyone else in your position wouldn't even try to set foot on the campus."

Mitzi hurried ahead and unlocked the door to Angie's apartment. Once inside Angie collapsed on her bed. Mitzi pulled the sheet over her daughter and tiptoed from the room. She smiled at Jay, trying to conceal her intense concern.

"I think she was asleep as soon as she hit the bed. She's emotionally exhausted. It will be no problem for me to spend the weekend with her. She's been through so much." Mitzi went to the kitchen and opened the refrigerator. "Jay, would you like a soft drink?"

"That sounds good," he replied, pulling up a chair to the kitchen table. "I only wish there were something I could do to help her."

Mitzi handed Jay a cold can of soda pop. "A good night's rest will be the best thing for her."

Mitzi slipped into a chair opposite Jay. Her face appeared ten years older than it did the week before. They sat in silence for a few moments, each enjoying their cold refreshment.

"I hope she'll be able to sleep the whole night through. I doubt if she's slept more than four hours in a row since the attack," Jay said as he studied Mitzi's wrinkled brow. "I wish I could stay tonight, but I have to be at work at midnight. My first sergeant has been more than understanding about letting me have time off, but the work is piling up."

"I appreciate all you've done for her. I don't know what we'd do without your help. I just hope Angie will be ready to start her new job."

Jay took the last sip from his can of pop, dropped it in the recycling bin, and walked toward the door. "She has ten days to go before she has to report to work. Hopefully, she'll be over this trauma by then. She's a strong lady." Jay hesitated as his large physique filled the door frame. "I'll call you tomorrow and see how she's doing."

Angie slept for most of the weekend. She would awaken for a few hours, her mother would fix her a warm, home-cooked meal, then she'd lie on the sofa to watch a little TV, only to fall asleep again. By Monday morning she was able to laugh at her own clumsiness when she dropped an egg on the kitchen floor while preparing breakfast.

"Mom, would you mind coming to the doctor's with me this morning? I still don't feel like driving."

"I'd be glad to. Afterwards, if you're feeling up to it, we could go by the college and get your diploma."

"As long as it's light outside, I think I'll be able to go back." Angie smiled as she finished her cheese omelet and carried her plate to the sink. "After all my hard work, I'd like to see that piece of paper. Maybe we could then go by the mall and get a frame for it. I want to have something positive to look at instead of my bruises and shaven head."

Mitzi gave her daughter a hug. "That's my old strong-willed daughter talking. Together we'll be able to conquer this."

"I'm tired of being miserable," Angie sighed. "I want to go back to what life was before the attack, but I know I can't. I don't understand why Jay keeps hanging around. He knows I'm damaged goods."

"Jay loves you for who you are. You have a very sweet spirit, and that is what attracts him. He knows that, regardless of what happened to your body, nobody can rape your soul."

"But, Mother, that man did rape my soul. I'm an emotional wreck. I've never cried so much in my entire life as I have these last few days."

"Your tears are a sign of your healing. They're a good thing, not a bad sign."

■ ■ ■ ■

Promptly at eleven-fifteen, Angie and Mitzi were ushered into the doctor's examining room. The nurse weighed Angie, took her pulse and blood pressure, and removed the bandage from her head. "Looks like your wound is healing well," she said. "The doctor will probably remove the stitches today."

"I hope so. They're beginning to itch."

After the nurse left the room, Angie turned to her mother. "I don't even remember what the doctor looks likes. That night in the hospital was such a blur."

"He's a graying Filipino. I thought he showed a great deal of professionalism and compassion."

Angie studied the degrees on the wall. "I'd feel a lot more comfortable if I had a female doctor."

"I wish we had a female gynecologist on Guam, but there just aren't enough women doctors who want to come here," her mother replied. "I've just accepted the fact that my doctor is going to be male. They're all well trained, but sometimes they don't have enough empathy for what a woman has to go through."

Suddenly, the door of the examining room

opened, and Dr. Cruz entered, followed by his nurse. "Angie, how are you doing?" he said as he extended his hand.

"I guess I'm as good as can be expected." Angie shuffled and gazed out the window. How could she possibly tell a strange man her innermost thoughts?

Sensing his patient's discomfort, Dr. Cruz turned his attention to her mother. "Hello, Mrs. Quinata. How have you been doing?"

"It's been extremely difficult for both of us. I'm concerned about Angie. She's unduly upset and doesn't seem to be bouncing back like I'd hoped."

"Oh, Mom," Angie sighed. "Just because I wasn't able to go to my graduation doesn't mean I'm a basket case. I'm going to be okay; I'm just tired."

"I know, Honey. I just can't bear to see you so unhappy."

A stern look crossed the doctor's face as he frowned at Mitzi. "Often it takes a lot longer for the inner pain and fears to heal than the physical. I can take care of the physical problems now. We can deal with the other later."

Mitzi nodded with resignation. *If only he understood a mother's heart. Many doctors are always too matter-of-fact and seldom hear our real pain.*

"Angie, let's take a look at your stitches. Hopefully, I'll be able to take them out today."

"I hope so," Angie replied as she removed her flowered scarf.

Dr. Cruz took her head in his hands. "Hmm. Looks like the stitches are ready to come out." He looked over his shoulder to his nurse who was already getting supplies from the cupboard. "Gloria, would you prepare a suture removal kit for me?"

Dr. Cruz's hands moved swiftly and confidently as one by one he snipped each of the twenty-five stitches in Angie's head. In a few moments he stepped back and beamed. "In a few days the cut will be completely healed. Of course with a wound that size, there will be a slight scar, but when your hair grows back, no one will ever know."

Angie smiled shyly. "Thank you, Doctor. I appreciate all you've done for me."

"You've been a brave patient, but before you go I'd like to take another blood test."

"I thought I'd been put through the entire gamut of tests while I was in the hospital."

"You were, but we had to wait a few days before we could perform this particular one."

"And what is it?" Angie asked softly.

"HIV."

Horror smothered Angie and Mitzi as they exchanged panicky glances. Neither one could speak for several minutes. Finally Mitzi gasped, "I never even thought about AIDS."

"I did," Angie whispered as tears filled her eyes, "but I was afraid to say anything. I was hoping that since they didn't take an HIV test at the hospital that I wasn't at risk. Jay would never get close to me again if he thought I had AIDS."

"There's such a small number of AIDS cases on Guam, the chances are good you were not infected. But let's not take any chances. It's best to be sure."

Mitzi's face remained ashen, while she watched the nurse draw blood from her daughter's arm. "I heard that tests sometimes don't turn up positive for months or even years after contact."

"That's true," the doctor replied. "That's why Angie should be tested every two or three months for the next couple years, or until the perpetrator can be found and tested for HIV."

"But the police don't have many clues to go on. The chances of finding him is practically nil. He probably caught the next plane out of here," Angie cried.

The doctor handed his patient a tissue

from the nearby counter and waited while she dried her eyes and regained her composure. "Angie, I wish I could talk with more certainty now, but I don't want you to take any risks. Until more research is done, the medical community cannot cure AIDS."

"So what should I do? Avoid other people?" Angie asked bitterly. "If anyone thought I had AIDS, they would avoid me, wouldn't they?"

Mitzi put her arms around Angie and drew her close. "It'll be okay," she whispered as she brushed Angie's hair away from her cheek. "God hasn't let us down before, and He won't let us down now."

Angie appeared not to have heard her mother, but the words sunk deep into her soul where they collided with a mass of anger, rage, and guilt. "I can't go on. I can't bear the thought of AIDS."

The doctor watched the mother-daughter exchange with concern. When both of them paused for lack of words, the doctor put his hand on his patient's shoulder. "Angie, I have a doctor friend who specializes in helping victims of rape. May I give him a call and set up an appointment?"

"Are you saying I'm crazy?" Angie's eyes blazed through her tears. "I don't need a psychiatrist. All I need is the assurance that

I didn't contract the HIV virus."

"Would you consider talking with him at least once?" the doctor persisted.

"I don't want to see any psychiatrists. If I thought I needed help I'd see my minister."

The doctor stroked his beard. "That might be one solution," he replied. "I don't know your particular minister. However, I do know that some are exceptionally well trained as counselors and others cause more harm than good. I hope yours is one of the well trained."

Angie took a deep breath and forced a smile. "I'll consider it," she murmured.

Dr. Cruz reached into a drawer beside him and took out a business card. "If you change your mind about seeing a professional, here's my friend's name and telephone number. He has an answering service so feel free to contact him day or night. He's always willing to help."

Angie studied the letters and numbers on the card, then tucked it into a corner pocket of her purse. *This is the last person on earth I'd call,* she told herself as she wrapped her scarf around her half-shaved head and rose to leave.

Mitzi and Angie drove the streets of Agana in silence. A coconut fell from the palm tree directly beside their car, yet neither reacted.

Their senses remained numb with shock. When Mitzi turned her car down the street to her daughter's apartment in Magnolia, Angie spotted Jay's car parked by the curb. "Mom, if you don't mind, I'd rather be alone when I tell Jay about the HIV test."

Mitzi's face softened as she stopped her car behind Jay's. "Of course, Dear. You two need to be alone. If you need anything, be sure and call me tonight."

"Mom, don't make such a fuss over me. I'll be fine."

"I know you will. I just want to help take your pain away."

"I know," Angie said as she opened the car door and spotted Jay hurrying toward her. "I'll talk to you later. Thanks for taking me, Mom."

"Hi," Jay greeted as he reached for his friend's hand. "What kind of good report did the doctor give you?"

Angie forced a smile and tried to add a tone of gaiety. "The stitches came out so now maybe I can wear my new wig. I'm getting tired of this silly scarf."

"That's my girl. I'm glad to see the old Angie back."

Angie unlocked the door to her apartment and motioned for Jay to follow her. "Can I get you a glass of iced tea?"

"I'd love it," he replied, leaning over to kiss her.

Angie jumped back in terror. "You can't do that," she shouted. Seeing the pain in Jay's eyes, she immediately regretted her reaction.

"What's wrong? I've always greeted you with a kiss. Have I done something?"

"I'm sorry. . . . I don't know if I'll ever be able to kiss you or anyone else again."

The grooves on Jay's forehead deepened. "Why's that?"

Angie felt a lump building in her throat. She had to be brave and not let Jay know how upset she actually was. "They tested me for the HIV virus this morning," she replied, trying to make her voice sound matter of fact.

Jay wrapped both his arms around her. "I'm sure it will come back negative."

"But maybe the tests don't show anything for months or even years after contact. I don't want to risk spreading the virus. I hope you understand." Angie's eyes pled for patience.

Jay again wrapped his arms around her and pulled her close. "Angie, you can't get AIDS from a simple kiss. It can only be spread by sexual contact, dirty needles, or tainted blood."

Angie shook her head vigorously. "Jay, I think too much of you to take any risks. Besides, I heard that you could get AIDS by any exchange of body fluids."

"Angie, there are so many rumors and false notions about AIDS floating around that you could live in total fear and isolation. As long as we have no proof, let's go on with our lives as if this had never happened. Hopefully, they'll find the attacker soon, and we will know for sure if he's infected or not."

Angie relaxed as she squeezed Jay's hand. "I'll do my best. Now how about the iced tea I promised you?"

CHAPTER 4

Angie adjusted her new hairpiece. *Not bad for a cheap wig,* she sighed. *Maybe I'll be able to hide my scars for a few months until my hair grows out. I'm going to wear this and try to forget that anything ever happened. Hopefully, no one saw the article in the paper. After all, it was hidden on the third page.*

She glanced at her clock radio. *Seven o'clock.* She paced nervously around the room. *I don't have to be at work until nine. I'd better recheck my supplies. It'd be embarrassing not to have everything I need. I don't want to appear like a novice, even if I am one.* For the next hour Angie counted her curlers, then arranged and rearranged her cosmetic box. She took out her class notes and compared her supplies with the recommended list. Everything had to be perfect.

Ten minutes before nine Angie walked into the Coiffure and Manicure Beauty Salon at the Agana Mall. She hesitated as she gazed around the mirror-lined walls. Angie had been in this salon several times as a customer when she was in high school, but now she was to be the one standing above the chair with scissors and curling iron in her hand.

As she stood there in awe, a dark-haired man emerged from the back room. "Hello, you must be Angie. I'm Yan Chung, the owner. I'm glad you could join our little family. You'll add a touch of class."

"Thank you." Angie blushed as she lowered her eyes. "I'm glad to meet you. Mr. Paplos, my teacher at the college, spoke very highly of both you and your salon."

"He's a great guy. That's why I take his best students, no questions asked."

He paused, his penetrating eyes drifted up and down Angie's trim body. "All my friends call me Yan. Here, let me take your box, and I'll show you around."

Yan carried Angie's box of supplies to the back of the salon and set it on the counter in front of a beauty chair. "I'll start you out here in the corner across from my office so I can help you whenever you need it. When you build up your clientele, I'll see that you move closer to the front windows. Your pay will go up in proportion to how well you produce."

Angie studied the area: sink, mirror, outlets, drawers, and carts. "Looks like I have more space than I could possibly use," she smiled. "I'll take a few minutes and unpack my things."

"There's plenty of time for that. Let me show you the beauticians' lounge." Yan put his hand on her shoulder and steered her toward the back door. Angie muffled a gasp as she stepped onto an Oriental rug in the posh lounge.

"My girls work hard so I try to give them the very best. You're free to keep whatever you'd like in the refrigerator and use the microwave. Of course, there's continual disagreement as to what to watch on the TV during the slow times."

"It's beautiful." Angie smiled. "Hopefully, I'll have enough business that I won't have much time to watch TV. I'm sure there'll be plenty of laundry and cleaning to do in my free moments." Angie surveyed the room. "Where does the background work take place? The cleaning supplies and the laundry?"

"You're a practical one." Yan snickered. "I told you I take good care of my girls. You won't have to worry about the menial tasks. I've hired a young immigrant for that. Her English is broken, but she's learning fast."

Suddenly, the bells on the door tingled, and Yan stuck his head out the door. "Hi, Sweetie. Come back and meet our latest addition. She's likely to double our business."

A beautiful Chamorro woman walked into the lounge. "Hi. I'm Tracy Ada. We're glad to have you here, but I hope you don't believe half of Yan's stories." She grinned as she winked at her boss.

Angie wrinkled her forehead with puzzlement, then smiled. "I'm glad to be here," she replied. "My name's Angela Quinata."

"It's nice meeting you. We need a new face around here. Life's getting a little boring."

"I've got some work to do so I'll leave you two to get acquainted," Yan said as he patted Tracy on the shoulder as he left the room.

"You've got to take him with a grain of salt," Tracy grinned. "He's all talk and little action."

"He does have a pretty strong come-on," Angie replied as she shrugged her shoulders and smiled. "But I met guys a lot worse while I was in college."

Angie and Tracy spent the next few minutes comparing their training background. One by one, four other beauticians joined them as the salon became busy with customers. Several beauticians were overbooked and were more than happy to schedule customers with Angie. On several occasions she spotted Yan in her mirror watching her work from his glassed office. *I wonder if he doesn't trust my work,* she mused. *Does he check up on all his new beauticians this way?*

At lunch time Angie had only a few minutes to eat a quick sandwich in the lounge before returning to her next haircut. The looks of pleasure on her customers' faces when they surveyed their finished hairstyles increased Angie's self-confidence.

She worked for several hours before the thoughts of her attack slipped into her consciousness. *If I discipline my mind and keep busy, maybe I'll be able to get over what happened on the campus,* she told herself during the moments when memories rose to torment her.

"Angie, you don't have to do a week's work on your first day." Yan grinned as he came out of his office and paused next to her chair. "It's after five; you won't be any good at all tomorrow if you don't go home and get some beauty rest. I bet you have someone special waiting for you."

Angie shrugged her shoulder and reached into the bottom drawer of her station for her purse. How should she answer? She'd given Jay back his ring, but regardless of how cruel she'd been to him, he was always there helping her as if she only had a case of the flu instead of having been ruined for life.

"I have a lot of special people in my life," she replied cautiously. "Have a good evening."

Angie gathered her things and turned to the other beauticians. "I guess I'll call it a day as well. I'll see you tomorrow."

"See ya," they responded in chorus as Angie left the air-conditioned salon.

The hot tropical wind slapped Angie in the face as she left the mall. She hurried across the parking lot. A tall, athletic man was walking toward his car in the next row. Angie ran to her car, slid behind the wheel, and locked the door. She laid her head on the steering wheel as her heart raced and her hands trembled. *Could he be the one?* Minutes passed as she watched the man climb into his car and drive away. Breathing a sigh of relief, she started her engine and headed toward her apartment in Magnolia. Her nearly perfect first day of work ended with an unwarranted scare.

Angie finished eating two hamburgers, potato chips, and reached for a chocolate bar. *Mother would be infuriated with me if she knew I was indulging in such junk foods,* she justified, *but after all I've been through, I deserve it. The added stress is probably burning up most of the calories so it won't add to my weight.*

As she stuffed the last bite of the chocolate morsel into her mouth, the doorbell sounded. She hurried to the door and paused. Her voice trembled, "Who's there?"

"Relax, Angie. It's just me," Jay shouted through the door. "I came to see how your first day of work went."

Angie flung open the door. "I'm sorry. Under the circumstances I just can't be too careful."

"Aren't you going to invite me in?" Jay teased.

"Of course. Come on in. Have you eaten yet?"

"I ate before I left the base. I'm not in the habit of turning up hungry on someone else's doorstep." Jay pulled out a chair at the kitchen table. He smiled and automatically reached into the bag of potato chips. "Now, tell me about your first day of work."

"I loved it. After all my months of training, I got a real adrenaline high from seeing the expressions on the ladies' faces when they saw how I changed their straight, disheveled hair."

"Women are so vain." Jay chuckled.

"Ah, come on. I was merely helping their self-esteem," Angie retorted lightly.

"How many did you do today?"

"I did one perm, three wash and sets, and I can't remember how many cuts. The other girls were all overbooked, so I was busy all day. It was great."

Jay reached for Angie's hand. "It's good to see you happy again. I knew you could do it."

Angie's joy was short-lived. She wrinkled her forehead. "The day wasn't entirely perfect," she sighed. "Yan, the owner, gives me the creeps. I can't quite put my finger on it, but there's something about him that bothers me."

"You're probably just gun-shy about all men. After all, it's only been less than two weeks since your attack."

Angie nodded her head. "I suppose you're right." The tone of her voice did not reflect the confidence in his voice. "He does seem to take good care of his employees. He has the fanciest beauticians' lounge I've ever seen. He's even hired a maid to launder the towels and clean up after us. It's nothing like what our textbook described."

"Don't knock a good thing when it happens." Jay chuckled. He glanced around the small apartment. "How about going to a movie to celebrate your successful day?"

"I'm not leaving this apartment when it's dark outside, even if I'm with you."

"Then how about me running to the video store and renting a couple of videos for the evening? I'll make sure they're comedies."

"That I can handle," Angie replied as Jay rose to leave. "If you want to get some snacks along the way, I could handle that too."

The pair spent the evening nestled on the sofa laughing at the latest antics from Hollywood. Angie was proud of how well she was able to suppress her pain and act as if everything was back to normal. Maybe if she masked her pain and anger, it would go away.

Four other beauticians were gathered in the lounge of Coiffure and Manicure the next morning when Angie arrived.

"Hi, Angie," Tracy greeted. "Have you seen the morning paper yet?"

"No. I've been running a little slow this morning."

"Another woman was raped at the college last night. The article said it was the sixth one in the last three months. I'd be scared to death to go near that place until that crazy has been caught."

Angie turned pale and slumped into a chair. Her heart pounded while her hands trembled.

"Angie, are you okay?" Tracy asked. "You look like you've seen a ghost."

Angie took a deep breath and scolded herself. *I've got to get control of myself. I don't want to blow it on my second day of work.* She forced a smile. "I'm all right. I live in that neighborhood, and I get extremely upset whenever that happens."

"I don't know why the cops can't figure out who it is," the blond beautician on the other side of Tracy said as she arranged her curlers in their tray. "I wonder if they really care about the plight of women."

Just then Yan appeared in the doorway. "I see you girls have seen the morning paper about the mad rapist. I'll tell you why the cops can't figure out who did it," he said with a strange gleam in his eye. "They're stupid." With that he turned and walked away.

The beauticians exchanged puzzled glances, shrugged their shoulders, and went to their individual stations to prepare for their day's customers. Angie shook her head as the others seemed to accept his attitude as a normal, off-the-cuff comment.

Angie could scarcely keep her composure as the latest rape was the chosen topic of conversation of nearly every woman who came into the salon that day. At three o'clock Grandma Santos entered the salon. Mrs. Santos lived just two blocks from the mall and frequently treated herself to a new dye job to hide her nearly gray head of hair. Everyone else was busy, and she was sent to Angie's station.

Angie helped her select an appropriate color and had just begun the process when Grandma Santos asked, "Young lady, did you read about the rapes in the paper?"

"Uh-uh," Angie mumbled. "It's pretty terrible."

"Well, if young girls today wouldn't run around half naked, they wouldn't be attacked. They ask for it every time they dress that way."

Angie's face reddened. "No one deserves to be raped. It's a violent crime against all women."

"If the truth were known, I bet some of those girls actually enjoyed it. That's why they choose to dress the way they do."

Angie slammed the dye bottle onto the counter, grabbed her purse, and ran from the salon.

"What got into her?" Mrs. Santos asked

Tracy, who was putting the finishing touches on a perm at the next station. "You'd think I personally attacked her or something."

"I don't know what's wrong," Tracy replied. "She's been acting strangely ever since she came to work today. Give me a few minutes, and I'll finish doing your hair."

"I hope Yan doesn't hear about this. He's always been fussy about who he picks to work here, but it looks like he picked a neurotic one this time. I guess it goes to show that you can't tell a book by its cover."

Tracy shook her head. "She's totally different today than she was yesterday. I don't know what got into her. The way she's been acting you'd think she was the one who was raped."

Angie ran to her car. She could scarcely see through her tears as she drove the familiar streets to her apartment. Her heart raced, and the blood vessels in her head pounded under her wig. *Oh, God, where are You?* she pleaded. *I can't take any more. Isn't there someplace I can go to get away from this?*

Parking her car, she breathed a sigh of relief when she recognized her mother's car in the visitor's spot. She hurried to her apartment. "Mom, how come you're here? How'd you know I needed you?"

Mitzi grinned as she hugged her daughter. "Mother's intuition. When I read the article in the paper today, I knew it was going to be tough for you. I didn't know how long you'd be able to last at work so I thought I should be here when you got home. I'm glad you gave me a key."

"Mom, it was awful. Everyone is either scared to death, or they think it would never happen to them. One of my customers thought it was the woman's fault. She got obnoxious, and I just couldn't handle it. I broke down and ran out of the shop leaving her in the middle of a dye job. I'll probably lose my job over it."

"Was your boss there at the time?"

"No, but I'm sure she'll tell him. Grandma Santos is not someone to reckon with. She'll go right to the top."

"If your boss asks you about why you left, why don't you simply tell him the truth? I'm sure he'll be sympathetic."

"Mother, you don't understand. I can't talk about it with anyone except you and Jay. And I don't understand how Jay can keep hanging around. Doesn't he realize I'm ruined for life?"

"If Jay can understand and stand behind you, I'm sure your boss will also understand once he knows what happened."

Angie sunk onto the sofa and reached for the box of chocolates she had left on the end table. She sighed as she took a bite from the candy. "If I'm going to lose my job, I might as well go out fighting."

"That's the spirit," Mitzi replied as she patted her daughter on the knee. "You'll see. Everything's going to work out. Just be patient."

The next day Angie walked into the Coiffure and Manicure Beauty Salon exactly at the appointed time. Yan had not yet arrived, and the other beauticians were already busy at their stations. "Hi, Angie. Are you feeling better today?" Tracy greeted.

"Much better, thank you," she replied as she put her purse in the bottom drawer. "I'm sorry I ran out yesterday. I just couldn't take any more of Mrs. Santos's comments. I assume she was pretty upset with me."

Tracy giggled. "She'll get over it. I finished her dye job. Fortunately, Yan wasn't here when she left so she didn't have an opportunity to tell him her side of what happened."

Tracy studied Angie's face. "I know I haven't known you for long, but is something wrong? Ever since you saw that article in the paper you completely changed."

"Tracy, have you ever been raped?"

"No."

"Then you'd never understand."

Their conversation was interrupted by the ringing of the phone. Tracy hurried to the front desk. She reached for the master schedule and recorded the caller's name and request, thanked her, and hung up. Angie busied herself by straightening her already immaculate work area.

"Angie, this customer specifically requested you," Tracy said as she handed a slip of paper to her. "She said you did her friend's hair, and she just loved it and wanted you to fix hers as well. For only having been here two days, I'd say you're off to a great start. They're already asking for you by name."

Angie worked all morning as if nothing had happened the day before. Yan came to the salon at eleven o'clock and went directly to his office without saying a word. Several times Angie noticed him watching her through his office windows, but he made no effort to contact her. *Maybe he doesn't know about what happened yesterday,* she mused as she again observed him in her mirror. *Leaving work was a dumb thing for me to do, but I just couldn't control myself.*

Angie was just saying good-bye to a customer when Yan approached her station. "Can I see you in my office for a few minutes?" he asked as he put his hand on her shoulder.

Angie's heart sank. *It's all over. . . . I'm being fired. . . . But if he were going to fire me, why didn't he do it when he first came in this morning?*

Yan closed the door behind them, then motioned for her to be seated. "I understand you had a little problem here yesterday."

Angie's eyes fell to the floor as blood rushed to her face. "I'm sorry. I won't let it happen again."

"What did Grandma Santos say that upset you so badly? She's been a customer of ours since we opened." Yan tried to project an air of concern, but a hollowness reverberated in Angie's ears.

"She was making a lot of unkind remarks about the rapes that have been taking place around the college. I just couldn't handle it. I'm afraid I lost control of myself."

"But the other girls heard them, and they didn't run out the door," Yan said as his dark eyes pierced deep into her soul.

Angie's palms began to sweat, and her voice trembled. "B-b-but they've never been raped."

"And you have?"

"Yes," Angie mumbled as her eyes stared on the sparkling tile at her feet.

Yan scrutinized the quaking young woman before him. His silence unnerved her even more. "Do you know who did it?"

"It was dark, and he knocked me unconscious first."

"It's over. You should just forget it and go on with your life. I know a perfect cure. I'll pick you up at seven o'clock; we'll go out to dinner, then have a little fun afterwards."

Tears filled her eyes. *Doesn't anyone understand what I'm going through? Going out is the last thing I want to do, especially with Yan.*

"I'm sorry, but I'm just not up to it tonight," she responded cautiously.

"It'll be good for you," Yan retorted. "You can't stay home and sulk about it. I'll show you what a good time is."

"Please, I'd prefer not."

"You like working here, don't you?"

"Yes."

"Then we need to get better acquainted," Yan whispered.

Angie took a deep breath. "I prefer to keep my career separate from my personal life."

Yan shook his head with disgust. "If that's the way you want it. Just remember your career could expand a lot faster if you made the right connections. This is a very competitive business."

"I'll remember that," Angie replied as she rose to leave, "but I prefer to make it in the hairdressing business strictly on my styling talents." She glanced nervously out the window and breathed a sigh of relief. "If you'd excuse me, my next customer just arrived."

"Customers do come first." Yan grinned. "But ten years from now you could still be working at the same station for the same pay if you don't begin to make social contacts."

Angie closed the office door, took a deep breath, pasted on a phony smile, and greeted her customer. She began to style her hair just the way she requested even though she personally thought the style was not suitable for her square face. Fortunately, the middle-aged woman carried on a monologue about her family, and Angie merely had to nod at the appropriate time.

When Angie finished, the woman admired herself in the mirror. "This is the best hairstyle I've ever had. I'm going to be back next week for you to do the same thing. Here's an extra ten dollars. You're worth every cent of it."

After the satisfied customer left, Tracy turned to her neighbor. "Angie, you're really starting off with a bang."

"She was rather generous, wasn't she?"

"No, I mean with Yan," Tracy replied. "Did he ask you out?"

"Yes. How'd you know?"

"He takes everyone who works here out. Usually he spends time sizing up his new employees and waits for at least a month to ask. He asked you the third day on the job."

"He said it would further my career, but I'd rather keep my personal life separate from my job."

"You're still a naive, fresh graduate. You'll soon learn Yan holds a key to big money." Tracy broke off her conversation as her next customer walked in.

Mystified, Angie checked the master schedule and noted she had no one else scheduled for the day. She took her purse from the bottom drawer in her station and slipped out the door. She still had her job, but something strange was happening that she didn't understand.

Angie stopped at the mall grocery store and bought a large frozen pizza, a six-pack of soda pop, and another box of chocolates. If the world was spinning out of control around her, she could at least treat herself to the foods she liked.

She hurried home, put the pizza in the oven, and sank onto the sofa, too depressed to even cry. *The first day Jay came to see how my day went. Yesterday mother was here, but tonight I'm on my own . . . me and the four walls.*

The buzzer on the oven timer broke her depressing fantasies. Angie took her pizza to the table. Within minutes she'd devoured the entire pizza, then reached for a chocolate for dessert. *I'd like to talk to Jay, but it's not fair to him. He deserves someone better than me. I returned his ring for a reason, but he still keeps coming around. He'd have fits if he knew Yan asked me out tonight.* She popped another piece of chocolate in her mouth. *I've already lost my purity and the best man on earth. Maybe I should find out what Tracy was talking about when she said Yan was the ticket to big money. If I made a lot of money, I could make a sizable donation to the church building fund. Making money couldn't be all bad. My life has already been destroyed.*

Angie went to bed early that night, but sleep escaped her. Life had been so good up until three weeks ago. She was graduating with honors, she had a mother who doted over her, she thought she had a faith in God that was unshakable, and the most desirable man on the island was interested in only her. Now she had a sterile diploma, a mother who couldn't understand her turmoil, a God that she was convinced had abandoned her, and a boyfriend she did not deserve. Life was scarcely worth living.

CHAPTER 5

Rebecca Hatfield's eyes surveyed the majestic Rocky Mountains that surrounded her town of Rocky Bluff. The inspiration of the rugged mountains and glimmering lakes of Montana had helped maintain her during her two years on Guam as a librarian. Now she was home for good with only her fond memories of the tropical island. A blanket of snow still glistened from its peak even though it was nearly the middle of the summer. *Nothing is more beautiful than the mountains of Montana,* she mused as she opened the door to the Looking Glass Beauty Salon.

Barbara Old Tail emerged from the back room as the bells on the door tingled. Her face broke into a broad grin. "Hi, Rebecca. It's good to see you again. It's been a long while."

"I've been working part-time at the florist shop, then I agreed to set up the county historical library. I didn't realize it would be such a task when I consented to do it, but I'm sure it'll be well worth my time when we're finished."

"I heard about your work from one of my clients, and I'm extremely excited about the Native American collection. It's something our community has needed for a long time," Barb said as she motioned for Rebecca to be seated in the stylist's chair.

"We should be done in a few weeks," Rebecca replied as she scowled in the mirror and fingered through her hair. "It looks like it's perm time again, doesn't it?" she chuckled.

"It has been several months since you've been in," Barb replied with a twinkle in her eyes. "I suppose your new husband has been filling up all your spare moments. How is Andy anyway?"

"He's doing great. They just broke ground for the new addition to the fire station, so he's been busy with the contractor and not home as much as when we were first married."

Barb tilted the chair backwards and rested Rebecca's neck over the sink and began running warm water over her hair. She added a palm of shampoo and began sudsing Rebecca's hair. "Andy's the best fire chief Rocky Bluff has ever had. He's had to take command of more than his share of crises. People are still talking about the hardware store fire and the night the Reed home burned. His fire prevention program is the best in the state," Barb said. "You must be very proud of him."

"I've been extremely proud of his accomplishments. I think supervising the addition will be his last major project before retiring. He's talking more and more about retiring to the golf course."

"I can't imagine Andy limiting himself strictly to the golf course. Are you sure you won't be taking another adventure to Guam or some other distant port?"

Rebecca shook her head vigorously. "I loved my two years on Guam, but that was enough adventure for me to last a lifetime."

For the next hour as Barb washed her patron's hair and wrapped it onto pink rollers, the pair discussed the people, climate, and education of Guam. Outside of a few vacations to the coast, Barbara had not been out of Montana, and she was fascinated with the tales of the Chamorro people. Being part Native American, Barbara Old Tail readily identified with a people who, although American, nevertheless struggled to maintain their culture's unique identity. Her mind drifted back to her aging mother on the Blackfoot Reservation near Browning.

"When Mother was in better health, she had trouble reconciling being both American and Indian. Now it's a case of struggling from day to day," Barb said as her voice faded into a whisper.

Rebecca studied the beautician's strained face. Her features portrayed only a faint hint of her mixed ancestry. "Has your mother been ill?"

Barb continued mechanically unrolling the curlers. She rarely shared her personal concerns with her patrons, but Rebecca Hatfield was different. She had compassion and wisdom rarely seen in a beauty salon. "Physically, Mom's been doing quite well for being nearly eighty years old. She's one of the oldest living members of the tribe, but our family has been living with a painful secret for the last few years."

"How lonely," Rebecca responded, not wanting to pry but, sensing the desperation in Barb's voice, wanting to do what she could to help. "Is there anything I can do to help?"

"I wish there were." Barb sighed. "We can't hide the fact any longer that mother was diagnosed with Alzheimer's disease three years ago. She refused to leave her home, so my brother has been driving thirty miles each day to check on her. This past year she has deteriorated so much that it'll be dangerous for her to stay by herself any longer. I'd like to bring her to Rocky Bluff to live with me, but she'd be by herself all day while I worked," Barb hesitated as she finished rinsing Rebecca's hair.

Rebecca waited in silence for her beautician to continue. "I wish there was some way I could turn this shop into a partnership so I could be more flexible, but it's just too small."

"Have you checked other possibilities?"

"The cost of renting space in the mall would be prohibitive, and I can't afford to build a place of my own so I kind of gave up hope."

Rebecca was never one to give up easily. Two years in another culture had sensitized her problem-solving skills. "I stopped at the café next door for dinner last night, and someone was saying that the gift shop on the other side of you might go out of business. If that's the case, maybe you could knock out part of the wall and combine the two areas."

Barb's face brightened. "If that's true, it could be an ideal situation. I'll go over and talk to Renee when I finish my last appointment today."

"Be sure and let me know what you find out," Rebecca responded. "I'm really interested in your growth potential. Rocky Bluff's short on good beauticians, plus I'd hate to have your mother living by herself much longer."

Barb finished styling Rebecca's hair just as her next customer walked in with her three-year-old child. Rebecca complimented Barb's work, wrote her a check, and hurried from the shop. She still had several errands to run, and she wanted to get home early so she could prepare an extraspecial dinner before Andy returned. Ever since they started construction, he was near exhaustion when he returned at night.

After devouring a rib steak, carrots, a baked potato, salad, and two pieces of cake, Andy gave Rebecca an appreciative kiss and collapsed into his recliner. He leaned back, took the remote, and began channel surfing. He soon settled on a football game but was asleep within minutes in spite of the intensity of the game.

Rebecca loaded the dishwasher, poured herself a glass of iced tea, took her favorite mystery book, and curled up on the sofa. Time stood still as she immersed herself in clues and deceitful antagonists. Just as a vital clue was being revealed, the ringing of the phone intruded into her world.

"Hello."

"Hello, Rebecca. This is Barb. You're a real genius."

The retired librarian shook her head and tried to shift mental gears from her novel. "How so?" she chuckled.

"I visited with Renee after work today, and she said they were closing down the end of the month. I immediately called the owner of the building, and he's coming by tomorrow morning to talk specifics."

"That's terrific," Rebecca nearly shouted, then lowered her voice as she noticed Andy stirring in his recliner. "I hope things can be worked out for you to expand."

"So far it looks good. Hopefully, I'll be able to remodel, but I'm afraid I won't have the time to do it and still keep my business going."

"I'd love to help you," Rebecca replied. "It would be a welcome change of pace from my work at the museum."

"You're an angel. I don't know how you find the time to do all you do."

Rebecca looked around her living room, remembering how horrified people were when she first bought the neglected, rambling house. After a lot of creativity and a little money, it was now one of the show-places in Rocky Bluff. She was energized just thinking about the possibility of redecorating a cold, sterile building. "Just tell me when to begin, and I'll be there," she laughed.

"If this goes through, it would probably take most of the rest of the summer to remodel. Hopefully, I'll be ready to hire another beautician by fall," Barb planned out loud. Her mind began to race. The longer she talked the faster her speech became. "I could then move Mother into my spare room before the snow flies."

"Sounds like you have everything all mapped out," Rebecca said as she brushed her graying hair from her forehead. "I certainly admire your forethought. I'm sure everything will turn out okay."

Barb took a deep sigh. "The remodeling will be the easy part," she said. "The hardest part will be to find a beautician who is pleasant, easy to work with, and won't demand a lot of money."

"You're right." Rebecca nodded. "Most new beauty school graduates expect a lot of money the first year on the job and want no part of small towns. It would take a unique young person to come here and be happy without the excitement of city life."

Barb hesitated. With all the problems she was facing, it was hard for her to keep her confidence high. Yet, somehow when she was pressed to the limits, she tapped an unknown resource. "The Lord hasn't let me down yet. So I'm sure the right person is out there someplace just waiting to be asked."

Angela Quinata screamed and bolted upright. Her sheets were soaked with perspiration. The impression of a man with deep penetrating eyes continued peering through the darkness at her. A coiled snake had reflected off the dark-haired stranger's right shoulder. She lay back on her pillow and sobbed. A dog began barking beneath her window. She ran to the kitchen, grabbed a chair, and propped it against the already double-bolted door.

Returning to her bedroom, she peered into the darkness. The dog was barking at a cat he had chased up the banana plant just outside her window. Normally she would have laughed at her own fears, but tonight was different. She returned to her bed, flopped across the sheets, and sobbed hysterically. Daylight seemed to never come.

When the first glimmer of sunlight slid

between Angela's blinds, she staggered to the kitchen, fixed herself a cup of instant coffee, and took three bonbons from their box. Slumping into a chair at the kitchen table, she buried her face in her hands. She had to manufacture enough courage to go to work, but that was still three hours away. Her mind drifted back to the evil stranger with a tattoo. The tattoo seemed permanently imprinted in her mind.

Angie reached for the envelope from Dr. Cruz that was lying on the counter. She unfolded the wrinkled page. Her hands trembled as she reread its frightening message.

HIV TEST — NEGATIVE.
PLEASE RETURN IN TWO MONTHS FOR ANOTHER HIV TEST SINCE THESE TESTS ARE NOT VALID FOR SEVERAL MONTHS AFTER EXPOSURE TO THE VIRUS.

Maybe I have the HIV virus. Maybe everything I touch will be contaminated. Maybe I shouldn't even go to work. Angela paced around her apartment like a caged lion. Her eyes fell upon her Bible on the end table. She picked it up and clutched it to her breast. Somewhere there had to be a sense of peace. She sunk onto the sofa and began thumbing the pages. She read a few familiar passages here and there. Finally she received enough internal strength to shower and dress for work. She took extra care with her makeup as she had to conceal the dark circles beneath her eyes.

"Good morning," Tracy greeted as Angie walked into the salon at five minutes after nine. "I hope you had a good night's rest. You were so stressed out when you left yesterday."

"I'm fine," Angie replied as she nervously rearranged her station. "I have a pretty full schedule today."

Angie mechanically got through the day. Her styling was flawless, and she was able to make appropriate small talk with each of her clients. Her movements became robot-like without feeling or emotion. At five o'clock she left the salon, picked up a TV dinner, chips, and a soft drink, and headed home. Food had become her only source of consolation.

After eating her TV dinner and snack foods, Angie flopped onto her sofa, grabbed her TV remote, and began mindlessly surfing the channels. Nothing attracted her interest. Just as she clicked off the remote, the phone rang. Angie jumped with fear even though nothing was there to frighten her, then relaxed as she reached for the phone.

"Hello."

"Hello, Angie. How are you doing?" Jay asked.

"I'm fine. How are you?" Angie's voice was dull and monotone.

"Angie, you don't sound well. Is something wrong?"

"No. I'm just tired."

"I'm sorry. I was hoping to come and see you tonight," Jay replied sadly.

"I'd love to have you come, but I plan to turn in early tonight. I was having nightmares last night and didn't get much sleep. What frightens me is that it was all so real."

"I wish there was something I could do for you. Would it help to talk about it?"

"I don't know," Angie sighed. "I relived the entire rape. In my dream I could see a snake tattooed on the attacker's right arm. Do you think seeing the tattoo in a dream is important?"

"It could be you're now recalling a repressed memory, or it could be just your mind playing tricks," Jay said cautiously. "However, I'd suggest you call Officer Santos and tell her about your dream. It won't be enough to convict anyone, but they need any clues they can get."

"I'd hate to call her. I don't like talking about it."

"I can understand why you'd feel that way, but I do think they need to know. Doesn't Officer Santos work the evening shift?"

"I think so. Maybe if I get my courage up, I'll call her before I go to bed."

"Good girl." Jay smiled. "I'm really proud of you. I know it won't be easy for you, but you have a lot of inner strength. How about going swimming with me at Tarague Beach Friday afternoon?"

"I'd love to," Angie replied.

"Good. I'll pick you up at about two."

The two visited for a few more minutes, then agreed to get together the next evening. Angie hung up the phone and took a deep breath. Did she really have the courage to call the police station?

Basking in Jay's encouragement, she reached for the telephone book. She found the non-emergency number and dialed it. The phone was answered after the second ring by a male voice. Angie's voice trembled as she asked for Officer Santos.

"Officer Santos," a female voice greeted.

"Hello, this is Angela Quinata. I think I

remember something more about my attacker, but I'm not sure."

"Any little bit of information will be helpful. We still don't have a lot to go on," Officer Santos replied.

Angie described her dream and the vividness of the snake tattoo. She explained she wasn't sure where her dream ended and reality began. At that point she felt silly and wished she hadn't called.

"Angela, I'm glad you called. As you know, that's not enough to convict anyone, but we'll keep our eyes open for men with tattoos. So far, outside of him having dark hair, that's all we have to go on. If you think of anything else, be sure and call me."

The days passed with marked similarities for Angie. The customers continued to be pleased with her work. Yan kept watching her from behind his glass office window, and she kept having nightmares about a dark-haired man with a snake tattoo.

On Friday Yan did not appear at work at his normal time, and by noon Angie became curious. Between customers she turned to Tracy. "Where's Yan today? Is he ill?"

Tracy wrinkled her forehead. "Angie, you're so naive. You'll have to learn that you don't ask questions about what goes on at

Coiffure and Manicure. Yan does his own thing. If you want to get ahead in the business, you have to go along with what he says without questioning. He sets his own hours."

Blood rushed to Angie's face as she shrunk into herself. "Sorry," she muttered. "I didn't realize."

Just then Yan walked into the salon and went directly to his office without speaking to anyone. Angie stood frozen in horror. Yan was wearing a beige tank top with plaid shorts. On his right shoulder was the tattoo of a coiled snake.

Yan's dark eyes pierced her haze as it settled on Angie's trembling body. She grabbed her purse and ran from the shop. A red Toyota screeched to a stop as she darted between the rows of cars.

Not knowing what to do, Angie started her car and turned down Marine Drive toward the police station. Perhaps Officer Santos could help her. Tears filled her eyes as she maneuvered through the traffic. If only Jay wasn't busy with his job until Saturday afternoon.

Angie parked her car in front of the Guam police station and raced up the steps.

Her heart pounded wildly.

"May I help you," a stern face asked as

she entered the building.

"I need to see Officer Santos," Angie's voice trembled.

"I'm sorry; she doesn't come on duty until seven o'clock. Can someone else help you?"

"I-I-I don't know. I just have some more information about the rapist near the community college. Maybe I should come back later."

"No, don't do that," the brisk officer replied as he rose from his desk. "I'll take you to someone else in that division."

He motioned for her to follow him down a dark hall into a back office. Another stern male officer was hunched over his desk. "Officer Aguigui, this young lady claims to have more information about the rapes." The officer then turned and disappeared down the same dark hallway.

"Please be seated, Miss," Officer Aguigui said as he reached into his desk and took out a tape recorder. "Do you mind if I record this?"

Angie took a deep breath. She had been through this before, but never with someone as expressionless as Officer Aguigui. "No problem," she answered.

Angie then proceeded to recount what she remembered about the night of her rape and her nightmares about the dark-haired man with a coiled snake tattoo. Then she added about how she had seen that same tattoo on her boss. Her voice trembled with each sentence. Officer Aguigui took notes while the tape continued to turn.

When Angie finished, he looked over his dark-rimmed glasses. "Is there anything else you'd like to tell me?"

"No."

"Thank you for coming. I'll pass this information on to Officer Santos. We will certainly take a hard look at Mr. Yan Chung — but we can't arrest someone because of what you saw in a dream."

"I understand," Angie muttered as she rose to leave. Her shoulders slumped as she hurried toward her car. *What if Yan followed me from the mall?*

She drove home through the side streets and alleys, always looking over her shoulder. Children played in the yards as chickens wandered free around the tin-roofed houses. Her love for the diversity of Guam battled the fear of Yan and the lack of police protection. She wanted to call her mother, but she knew what her response would be . . . move back home with her. Angie was determined to be her own person and solve her own problems, regardless of how difficult they might be.

Angie hurried into her apartment and double-bolted her door. Breathing a sigh of relief, she hurried to her refrigerator. She took out a bowl of leftover Chinese noodles and popped it into the microwave. Within minutes she was relaxing in front of the TV, consoling herself with food. She vowed she would not let the events of the day haunt her until she talked with Jay. Her entire career as a beautician was on the line.

An hour before Jay was scheduled to arrive, Angie reached into her drawer for her swimming suit. The thought of spending an afternoon at Tarague Beach with Jay thrilled her. Tarague Beach was the nicest one on the island. Located on Andersen Air Force Base, only military personnel and their guests were allowed to use it.

She pulled on her aqua-and-blue-striped swimsuit and examined herself in the mirror. A look of horror spread across her face. Extra rolls of fat padded her normally petite five-foot two-inch frame. She threw herself across her bed and sobbed. Her mother's warning kept flashing through her mind. *Honey, you're not tall enough to add even a few extra pounds. You better watch your diet. You're eating more junk foods now than ever before in your life.* She lay on her bed and berated herself for gaining so much weight.

In the midst of her grief, the doorbell rang. She hurriedly tied her swimsuit wrap around her waist, dried her eyes with a tissue, and ran to the door. "Is that you, Jay?" she shouted through the bolted door.

"Who are you expecting?" he teased.

Angie opened the door and motioned for him to enter. "Hi, Jay. I'm glad you came, but I'm afraid I can't go to the beach with you."

Jay studied Angie's red, puffy eyes. "Why not? We've been planning this for days."

Tears again filled Angie's eyes. "I-I-I just can't. I look terrible."

"You look lovely," Jay assured her. "Your scarf looks like what all the other women are wearing at the beach."

"It's not my hair," Angie protested. "It's my new fat. I can't let anyone see me this way."

Try as he might, Jay could not convince her to wear a bathing suit to the beach. He finally convinced her to wear a pair of slacks and just enjoy the warm trade breeze while they watched the setting sun together.

Angie relaxed in the seat next to Jay as they drove toward the gate of Andersen Air Force Base. Maybe she was silly about being so upset over a few extra pounds. After all, if she exercised and watched her diet again, she could lose those pounds in a few weeks. She reached for the radio dial in Jay's car and settled on a local, popular station. Her spirits lifted slightly as her favorite love song echoed through the car. As the song ended, an excited announcer came on the air.

"And now for some late-breaking news," the announcer shouted. "The Guam rapist was apprehended as he attacked his thirteenth victim in the vicinity of Guam Community College. Officials will hold a press conference in the police station conference room at six o'clock. Please stay tuned for more details."

CHAPTER 6

Angie Quinata took a deep breath as Jay opened the front door of the Guam Police Station for her. Her desire to learn the truth of the Guam rapist was only slightly stronger than the fear of having to relive that horrible night.

"Angie, I'm glad you came," Officer Santos greeted as the young couple entered the reception area. "I've been trying to get ahold of you all afternoon. I need to talk with you before the press conference."

Angie shuddered, then forced a smile. "Why do you need to see me? I told Officer Aguigui all I knew."

Officer Santos patted Angie on the shoulder. "Relax. Everything's going to be all right."

"I'm sorry," Angie stammered. "I'm scared."

The police officer smiled and put them both at ease. "Come with me, and I'll fill you in on the details. Your friend may come too, if he'd like."

Angie looked at Jay for reassurance. He nodded his head and smiled. "Soon this will all be over for you."

The trio entered a small, glassed-in room with a large wooden desk, an upholstered executive chair, and three smaller chairs. Officer Santos arranged the guest chairs in a semi-circle and gestured for them to be seated. "I'm sorry I wasn't here when you came in yesterday. I listened to the tape of your interview with Officer Aguigui. It must have been a grueling experience for you."

"He was so harsh. I didn't think he understood what I was trying to tell him."

Officer Santos gave an understanding nod. "Men aren't often very sensitive about emotional issues."

"That's an understatement," Angie sighed.

"He understood a lot more than you realized. He got right to work on your lead just as soon as you left the police station. He had an immediate surveillance put on Yan Chung. Fortunately, we were there when he snuck up behind his next victim and tried to drag her into the bushes."

Those words calmed Angie's fears. She gradually unclutched her fists, and the wrinkles on her forehead faded.

Officer Santos studied the faces of the handsome couple across from her. *They've been through so much together. I wonder if this will be the end of their friendship? Few relationships survive such ordeals.*

Angie breathed a sigh of relief and took Jay's hand. "So I wasn't wrong after all. I was afraid the snake tattoo was just a dream and that I might be ruining an innocent person's life with my neurotic fears."

"Angie, don't be so hard on yourself. Repressed memories often surface in the form of a dream," the police officer explained. "That's why we were willing to take a chance and follow your lead."

"Do you think Yan has AIDS?" Angie blurted. "I have to have HIV tests for years to come, and I'm afraid to get close to anyone."

"We did some preliminary testing on Yan today, and one was the HIV test. We should have the results back in a few days."

Jay squeezed Angie's hand. "As soon as those tests are back, your fears will be over."

"It's not all that easy," Angie protested. "Even if I don't have HIV, I'm still a spoiled woman."

The hard, professional look faded from Officer Santos's face. "You remind me of my own daughter. She had a gentle spirit much like yours. She always put the needs of others over herself. We lost her in a diving accident a couple years ago." Silence enveloped the room as tears welled in the police officer's eyes. "Angie, I know it doesn't feel like it right now, but you're not a spoiled woman. You may have been physically harmed, but no one can damage your spirit."

"That's what I've been trying to tell her ever since this happened, but she doesn't and won't listen to me. I feel so helpless," Jay said.

"Jay, I know you want to protect her and make everything right for her, but this is a very individual experience for a woman. Those who have been violated respond best to other women who have been through the same thing. The emotions involved are hard to explain unless you've experienced it yourself. Rape is not something you can recover from overnight."

"Thank you," Angie whispered as she continued staring at the floor. "I'm glad someone understands what I'm going through."

Just as quickly as it had vanished, the professional side of Officer Santos reappeared. She glanced nervously at the clock over the young couple's heads and jumped to her feet. "It's almost time for the news conference; perhaps we can talk more after it's over."

The conference room was crowded with cameras, microphones, and reporters with tape recorders when Angie and Jay found a seat in the back row. Angie scanned the room nervously. *I hope no one recognizes me. What if they ask me questions? I could never speak in front of all these people.* She fidgeted in her chair as the Guam police chief walked to the podium.

"Welcome to this impromptu press conference," the chief said as he scanned the room. "It is with mixed emotions that I address you at this time. Fear has engulfed all the women on the island since the rapes began near the community college this past spring. Thirteen cases have been reported to the police department, and probably more than that have not. Many women are afraid to report such crimes and live the rest of their lives in fear and shame."

If I hadn't been beaten and taken to the hospital, I don't think I'd have had the courage to report the attack, Angie told herself. *It's all too embarrassing.*

The police chief's eyes settled on Angie's trembling lips. "Thanks to a tip from a brave young victim, we were able to locate the

115

suspect and apprehend him just as he was attacking another woman. We have arrested Mr. Yan Chung, owner of the Coiffure and Manicure Beauty Salon, and charged him with thirteen counts of rape. We are also investigating allegations that he ran a drug and prostitution ring from his salon. We expect to announce further arrests in the near future. I can't divulge details that would impede our ongoing investigation, but I'm willing to entertain any questions at this time."

A flood of hands flew up around the room. The police chief pointed to a reporter from a local TV station who had raised his hand. "Who was the woman who provided you the tip which led to the arrest of Yan Chung? What kind of information did you have to go on?"

Angie took a deep breath. *Please, God, don't let him say my name. I want to get as far away from Guam as possible. I don't want to be the subject of island gossip.*

The chief glanced at Angie's closed eyes and wrinkled forehead. He hesitated, then turned his attention back to the reporter. "I'm sorry, but that information is confidential. We must respect the privacy of the victims."

The maze of questions that followed were

a blur to Angie. It was all she could do to keep from running from the room. Her entire life lay in ashes around her. She was a spoiled woman, her place of employment was being investigated as a center for drugs and prostitution, and her reputation was ruined.

When the press conference was over, Angie and Jay merged with the crowd noisily rushing toward the front door. The last rays of the soft pink sun were setting over the Philippine Sea. The palm trees were still in the oppressive tropical heat. Angie was unaware of people scattering to their cars in the parking lot. She felt numb from head to toe. *I must be having a dream. This can't possibly be happening to me. Soon I'm going to wake up and be back in college planning for my graduation and applying for jobs.*

Angie sat quietly as Jay drove the familiar streets of Agana and turned toward Magnolia. There seemed to be no escape. Tears streamed down her cheeks as they neared her apartment. She took out a tissue and wiped her eyes.

Jay reached over and took her hand. "Honey, what's wrong? You should be happy; it's over."

"It will never be over for me," Angie snapped. "My reputation's shot. Even if the public never knows about the rape, everyone knows I worked for Coiffure and Manicure. I wish I could get as far away from Guam as possible. If I had relatives on the mainland, I'd be on the next plane out of here."

"You have a lot of friends in Montana," Jay replied. "Let me make a few calls tonight, and I'll get back to you tomorrow. You might begin mentally packing your bags. I'm confident I can work something out for you."

"No one will want an unemployed, penniless misfit," Angie objected bitterly. "Why should they care about my problems? They don't even know me."

"Rebecca Hatfield thinks the world of you. She's been writing almost twice a week asking how you're doing. I'll call her tonight and explain what has happened. There is plenty of healing love in Rocky Bluff."

Barbara Old Tail laid down her brush and wiped the perspiration from her forehead with the sleeve of her paint-splattered shirt. "I'll be glad when this heat wave breaks. If I thought it'd do any good, I'd get a bigger air-conditioner now, but there's just not enough summer left to make it worth my while."

"We're just about finished," Rebecca Hat-field said as she reached for her glass of iced tea. "You can be mighty proud of this extension. Hopefully, you'll be ready for customers by the first of September."

"I may have all the structural changes made by then, but I don't know where I'll find someone to help. I called the beauty schools in both Great Falls and Billings, and none of the graduates were interested in coming to Rocky Bluff. I'm getting plenty discouraged."

"There must be someone out there who's just right for your salon. God wouldn't have brought you this far to let you down now," Rebecca reminded her.

Barb shrugged her shoulders and grinned. "I know you're right. I guess I get discouraged too easily." Barb stepped back and surveyed the room that was once the Genteel Gift Shop. "I think I need to trim this with floral wallpaper. Would you like to go to Great Falls with me tomorrow and help me select wallpaper and mirrors?"

"I'd love to," Rebecca replied lightheartedly. "Andy is so busy with the addition at the fire station I doubt if he'll even miss me."

"Now that's talking like a true married woman," Barb chuckled. "How about if I pick you up around nine o'clock in the morning?"

Rebecca readily agreed, and the two women turned their attention back to the task before them. They added the final touches of paint to the room, then hurriedly cleaned their brushes. They were both eager to get home to prepare dinner for their spouses.

While Rebecca and Andy were relaxing over a bowl of sherbet after dinner that evening, their telephone rang. "Oh, no," Andy groaned. "I hope I don't have to go back to the station tonight. I was looking forward to a quiet evening at home with my bride."

Rebecca patted him on the shoulder as she hurried to the phone. "Hello," she said as she pushed her graying hair away from her ear.

"Hello, Rebecca," a deep male voice greeted. "How are you doing?"

"I'm doing great," she replied with a look of puzzlement. Suddenly her face brightened. "Is this Jay Harkness?"

"I knew you could never forget me," he teased. A wave of Montana homesickness swept over him, followed by a vision of Angie's troubled face. "How's life in Rocky Bluff?"

"Busy," Rebecca replied. "Andy's been putting in long hours at the fire station, and I've been busy helping Barb Old Tail remodel and expand her beauty salon. The physical plant is almost complete, but she's having trouble finding a beautician who's willing to come to Rocky Bluff to work for her."

Jay's heart began to pound. "Rebecca, could this be providence in action? Angie's begging to leave Guam, but she doesn't have any relatives on the mainland. She's been sheltered all her life. She doesn't know how to apply for a job, much less get set up on her own in a strange place. Do you think Barb would be interested in hiring Angie?"

Rebecca squealed with delight. "Angie would be perfect for her. I'm going to Great Falls with Barb tomorrow, and we'll discuss it then. I'll also talk with Andy about her staying here with us. We've remodeled the basement so she'd have her own private bedroom, bath, and sitting room. Why is Angie so anxious to leave Guam? She never seemed like the adventuresome type to me."

Jay shook his head with frustration. "Rebecca, it's the most unbelievable story. I'd have trouble believing it myself if I wasn't living it right along with her. Yesterday they arrested her boss for at least thirteen rapes in the vicinity of the community college. If that's not enough, they believe the place where she worked was the center of a prostitution and drug ring. She's in a deep state of depression."

"How terrible," Rebecca gasped. "That's reason enough for her to come to Rocky Bluff. I'd like nothing better than to take her under my wing and love her out of this. Give me twenty-four hours, and I'll see what I can work out. Will you be home tomorrow at this time so that I can call you back?"

"I'll be waiting anxiously for your call," Jay sighed. "Thanks so much. The people of Rocky Bluff have never let me down."

Rebecca hung up the phone and joined her husband in the living room. Even though they had been married just a little over a year, she was confident he would welcome a long-term houseguest. She and Andy talked late into the night. Andy had met Angie briefly on his visit to Guam before he and Rebecca were married. He remembered her merely as a shy Chamorro girl with an infectious giggle ready to burst forth at any time. The newlyweds planned how they would rearrange the basement so Angie could have privacy and comfort. As a confirmed bachelor for many years, Andy now looked forward to having a home bursting with the life and enthusiasm of a young person. He did not know, though, how deeply disturbed Angie really was.

Promptly at nine o'clock the next morning, Barb Old Tail stopped her black Mercury in front of the Hatfield residence. Rebecca grabbed her sweater, kissed Andy good-bye, and hurried to the waiting car.

"All ready?" Barb greeted.

"Couldn't be more so," Rebecca chuckled as she slid into the passenger seat and fastened her seat belt. "And do I have news for you."

"What's that?"

"Jay Harkness called last night and said his Guamanian girlfriend would like to come to Rocky Bluff to live for awhile."

"That's nice," Barb replied politely. "I suppose she'll stay with Bob and Nancy?"

"No, we both agreed that it would be better if she stayed with Andy and me," Rebecca could scarcely hold back her enthusiasm as her words began to fall over each other. "The best part is that Angie is a trained beautician right out of the School of Cosmetology at Guam Community College."

"She's a what?" Barb exclaimed as a rush of adrenalin shot through her body.

"A beautician . . . just what you've been praying for these last few weeks. And you were ready to give up hope," Rebecca exclaimed.

Barb's hands tightened around the steering wheel. "I can't believe it," she gasped. "I honestly thought I wasn't going to be able to get anyone. How soon is she going to come?"

"I have to call Jay back tonight with an answer. Are you certain you want to hire her? You know she does come from a slightly different background."

"Don't be silly," Barb chided. "Of course I do. In fact, it'll be fun having her. I'll start making plans for her to get her Montana Beautician's License right away. It shouldn't be too difficult since she graduated from an accredited cosmetology school."

"Then it's settled," Rebecca said. "I'll call Jay and tell him to buy the plane ticket. She'll probably come in a couple weeks since you usually get the cheapest fare with a fourteen-day notice."

The day flew by for the two friends from Rocky Bluff. They excitedly went from store to store looking for the perfect wallpaper for the salon. Knowing that she would soon have help added even more enthusiasm to Barb's shopping spree. God was answering

124

her prayers far better than she had ever anticipated. Instead of preparing a Montana girl to come to Rocky Bluff, the long arm of the Lord had reached half the world away.

In that place half the world away, Jay could no longer stand the suspense of waiting for Rebecca's call. He dialed Rebecca from Angie's apartment. After he and Rebecca talked for a few minutes, he handed the phone to Angie. "Rebecca, how can I ever thank you?" she said with tears running down her face. "I hate to leave Guam. It's the only place I've ever known, but I can't stay here," she sobbed. "I'll never be able to get another job. Being employed at Coiffure and Manicure is fatal to have on my resume. Everyone knows about the charges against them. But I don't want to impose on you and Andy."

"Don't be silly," Rebecca protested. "We're looking forward to having you. You'll love Rocky Bluff and all the people here."

"I've heard so many good things about it," Angie replied as she wiped the tears from her eyes and began to calm herself. "I'm anxious to meet all of Jay's family, especially his grandmother. She sounds like quite a lady."

"She's one of a kind. She's the matriarch

and mentor of nearly the entire community. She has a way of taking everyone under her wing and erasing the pain, regardless of how deep it might be."

Angie's eyes became distant as she gazed through the living room window at the palm trees below. "I need someone to erase the pain," she murmured.

Jay spent as much time as possible with Angie before she was to leave. He tried to describe the rolling plains and the nearby majestic snowy mountains. Nothing could ever replace his love for Montana.

"Angie, I wish I could be with you to experience the changing of the seasons. It's something words cannot describe. One day the leaves on a tree are solid green, and nearly overnight they become vibrant with oranges, yellows, and reds."

"It sounds beautiful," Angie replied as she slid closer to him on the sofa. "I stopped at the library this afternoon and thumbed through the travel books and magazines about Montana. It's so different from the cowboys and Indians that I pictured from the old westerns on TV. I can hardly believe that a week from today I'll actually be there."

Jay continued describing his hometown,

then made a list of all his family and friends that he wanted Angie to be sure and meet. She watched in awe as one name after another was added to the list.

"You can't possibly expect me to remember all these people," she protested good-naturedly.

"It won't take you long," Jay assured her. "Rocky Bluff is a close-knit, friendly community."

The ringing of the phone interrupted their lively conversation. Angie grudgingly picked up the receiver. "Hello."

"Hello, Angie?" a business-like woman's voice greeted. "This is Officer Santos."

Angie's face blanched. *I thought all of this was over and I'd never have to talk with the police again.* "Hello, Officer Santos," she answered politely. "What can I do for you today?"

A warm chuckle echoed over the phone wires. "Angie, relax. I just called to give you some good news."

The young woman breathed a sigh of relief. "And what is that?"

"Yan Chung's blood tests just came back. You'll be glad to know that he tested HIV negative." Officer Santos hesitated and waited for a response from the other end of the phone lines. Hearing none she continued, "You no longer have to worry about having AIDS."

Angie exploded with excitement. "Thank you. Thank you," she shouted. "I can go to Montana without fear of carrying AIDS. Thanks so much for calling."

"Good-bye and good luck," Officer Santos replied as Angie hung up the phone and turned to the handsome airman standing beside her.

"Now you'll no longer have an excuse not to kiss me," he chuckled as he took her in his arms, and their lips touched with sheer relief.

The last few days Angie and Mitzi tearfully sorted through Angie's things. It was difficult deciding what to ship to Montana and what to store at her mother's. Each article of clothing or household knickknack held a special memory.

"Are you sure I can't convince you to move back home?" Mitzi persisted as she taped shut still another box of clothing. "You're too young to be going halfway around the world by yourself."

Angie's eyes blazed. "I'm not a child anymore. Besides, I'm going where I'll have friends."

"That's the only redeeming part of this

whole deal," Mitzi sighed sadly. "I know Rebecca will take good care of you, but it's so far away. If you'd only wait a few months, everyone will forget about the arrests at Coiffure and Manicure. Any salon on the island would love to have a beautician with your talent."

"Oh, Mother. You're just prejudiced," Angie protested meekly. "There's nothing special about my talents. I just do what I was trained to do."

"You are a very special person," Mitzi persisted, "and I'm going to miss you."

Angie's face softened as she studied her mother's countenance. She noticed a few extra gray hairs and added wrinkles in her forehead. "I'll miss you too," she said as she leaned over to give her mother a hug. "I hope you'll be able to come and visit me. You've always said you'd like to visit Montana sometime."

"As soon as your plane lifts off from the airport, I'm going to begin saving my pennies to go. I've never seen snow before, so maybe I'll try to come during Christmas vacation. Just remember my love and prayers will always be with you wherever you may be."

"Thanks, Mom," Angie replied. "I need all the prayer support I can get. I'm really scared, but this is something I know I have to do. I hope you'll understand why I must leave Guam. It's not that I don't love you and don't want to share my life with you."

"As much as I'll miss you, you'll go to Montana with my blessing and all my love," Mitzi said as she hugged her only daughter, while tears streamed down her face.

CHAPTER 7

Rebecca Hatfield was overjoyed to spend a few hours with Edith Dutton. She hadn't seen her dearest and best friend for several weeks, and it was good to bask in her warmth again. She relaxed on Edith's sofa and told her of the recent telephone conversation she had with Jay Harkness and of the trauma that had befallen his girlfriend. She also told Edith of her friendship with Mitzi Quinata, the girl's mother, during her years in Guam. The former librarian vividly related the details that led up to her introducing Mitzi's daughter to the young airman from her hometown in Montana and the pleasure in watching their friendship develop.

Finally, Rebecca became even more intent in the conversation. "Edith, would you like to ride to Great Falls with me Wednesday to meet Angie's plane? It's a long drive to make alone."

"I'd love to," Edith Dutton replied excitedly. "I can hardly wait to meet her, but I'm afraid I won't be able to keep up with you. Maybe you should find someone else to go with you."

"I plan to make this a relaxing trip with a lot of stops in the rest areas. We have a lot of catching up to do," Rebecca answered. "I've been so busy helping Barb Old Tail expand her salon that I haven't had time to stop for my regular cup of coffee with you."

"I'd be lying if I said I didn't miss our coffee times together. I was having my hair done at the Looking Glass yesterday, and I have to congratulate you and Barb for a job well done." Edith smiled. "The entire Harkness family is extremely grateful for all you're doing to help Jay's friend. If I were ten years younger, I'd love to take her under my wing myself."

"You took more than your share of troubled young people under your wing," Rebecca replied with a twinkle in her eye. "It's time to let the rest of us do our part."

"It's hard for me to slide into the background," Edith chuckled. "Nancy and I would like to host a buffet dinner Sunday afternoon. That way everyone can meet Angie."

"That's extremely thoughtful of both of

you, but Angie is such a shy person I'm afraid it might be overwhelming for her."

"I've considered that," Edith replied. "That's why I thought I'd invite Dawn and some of her friends to have lunch with Angie on Saturday. I suggested that they pick out a comedy video to watch that afternoon to help break the ice. That way Angie could meet Jay's sister and several young people her own age in a more relaxed setting."

"I hope our good intentions aren't too much for her. I keep forgetting she's just been through an extremely traumatic experience. But, hopefully, if she's busy the first few days she's here, she'll be off to a good start of putting her past well into the past. Angie's a delightful girl," Rebecca replied, "but judging by Jay's description, she's pretty well traumatized. It may take us quite awhile to love her out of this."

"If there's one thing Rocky Bluff has plenty of," Edith chuckled, "it's love."

Rebecca leaned back in her chair and stretched. "I imagine Angie's going to be exhausted by the time she gets in. Why don't we make motel reservations in Great Falls, then show her some of the local sights before we drive home."

"Sounds great," Edith nodded. "In fact, it might be a good idea for us to do some serious wardrobe shopping with her. Winter's going to be upon us in a few weeks, and all she'll have will be clothes for eighty-five-degree weather. Since you'll be providing a place for her to stay, the least I can do is provide a winter wardrobe."

"Things are falling into place much easier than I first expected. If Angie only knew what she was coming into, she wouldn't be nearly as fearful as Jay says she is." Rebecca glanced at the clock over the kitchen sink. "I suppose I better be heading home in a few minutes. I still have a lot of housework to do. Tomorrow I'm going to go to Browning with Barbara and help move her mother to Rocky Bluff."

"How is her mother doing?" Edith asked.

Rebecca shook her head sadly. "Alzheimer's disease is ravaging her life along with those who love her. She's fortunate that she has a family that can nurse her during her failing years. Many Alzheimer's patients end up facing a confusing world alone and neglected."

"I'm fortunate that Alzheimer's is one disease that has passed me by," Edith said. "Even though my heart condition has been very frustrating at times, at least my mind keeps functioning."

"I hope scientists come up with a cure for

that disease soon," Rebecca said as she stood to leave. "It's a shame people who've lived vibrant, wholesome lives have to spend their last years in a state of mental deterioration. No wonder depression is so common among its victims."

Edith nodded her head knowingly and walked her friend to the door. They bade each other good-bye, and Rebecca hurried home to finish preparing Angie's room. She and Andy, along with Edith Dutton, shared a common conviction that with the combined efforts of the entire community of Rocky Bluff, Angie could be restored to her former self.

Angela Quinata bit her lip as she hugged her mother and Jay. She tried her hardest not to show how frightened she was as she headed toward the ramp of the Hawaiian Airlines 747. She had been to the airport many times before as she waited for friends who were arriving or leaving the island, but she had never flown herself. The passengers around her pushed confidently toward the doorway as their boarding section was called. Angie was swept along with the crowd into an unknown future.

"Welcome aboard," the trim, dark-haired flight attendant greeted.

Angie surveyed the rows of seats. She had seen scores of airplanes on TV, but being on one was totally different. Everyone seemed to know exactly where to go and what to do. "Hi," Angie said timidly. "I've never flown before. Where do I sit?"

"Let me see your ticket," the attendant replied kindly.

Angie handed her the ticket. The attendant studied the ticket, then looked down the aisle. "You have seat twelve A. Do you see the lady in the flowered dress?"

Angie nodded. The attendant smiled as she continued. "You'll be beside her, next to the window."

The frightened young girl clutched her bag and inched her way down the aisle. She stuffed her bag into an empty bin above her seat and turned to the lady in the flowered dress. "Excuse me. I think that's my seat by the window," Angie said as she stepped in front of the woman.

Her neighbor watched Angie nervously become familiar with her surroundings. "Is this your first trip off the island?" the older woman queried.

"Yes, it is," Angie murmured.

"I remember how frightened I was the first time I left the island. That was more than thirty years ago. Now I've been back and

136

forth to the mainland at least once a year, so it's getting to be a rather boring routine."

Angie became entranced watching the ground crew go about their normal preflight duties. She even thought she spotted her new set of luggage on the baggage cart which had just parked under her window. Her excitement soon faded as her eyes drifted to the reflective glass of the terminal. Behind those windows were the two major loves of her life, her mother and her boyfriend. Tears filled her eyes. *Will I ever see them again? Will I ever be able to return to Guam?*

Angie watched the island of Guam become smaller and smaller until it was a mere speck surrounded by miles of water. The screen rolled down in the aisle, and a dated thriller appeared. In sheer boredom, Angie reclined her seat, closed her eyes, and dozed off. Sleep was a welcomed release from her fears of flying into the unknown.

The eight-hour flight to Honolulu seemed endless; the movies and airline meals did little to make the miles pass quickly. Only conversation with the lady in the flowered dress beside her made the trip bearable.

"Where are you going?" the woman asked kindly.

"I'm landing in Great Falls, Montana;

then a friend is driving me to Rocky Bluff," Angie replied. "I have to change planes in Honolulu, then Seattle. My boyfriend tried to explain how to find out which gate my next plane leaves from, but I'm afraid I'll get on the wrong plane or get lost in the terminal and

Her ne_____ _____ _____ _____ on't worry about a thing. I'm on my way to Seattle myself. I'll make sure _____ _____ the right plane to Great Falls."

"I'd appr__ __te that, but I can't expect a total stranger to take that much time in helping me," Angie protested.

The lady in the flowered dress burst into a lusty laugh. "My name's Rose Chargalauf. I'm a professor at the University of Guam during the school year; then I teach classes at the University of Washington during the summer. We'll be sharing a limited amount of space for at least eleven hours, so we'll no longer be strangers when we get there. I'd be glad to help you through the terminal."

Angie giggled, then introduced herself, but when Rose asked her what she was going to be doing in Rocky Bluff, Montana, Angie blanched. *What can I say? I can't tell her I'm trying to get as far away from Guam as possible because I'd been raped and my*

138

place of employment is under investigation for drug and prostitution violations.

Angie's mind raced. Words tumbled out on top of each other. "I was offered a job in a salon in Ro___ Bluff, Montana. I don't know how long ___.

Rose wrinkled ___ ___ "Why did you choose Montana ___ ___ ___ that it gets real cold the___

"My high school l___ ___ s there, and she was able to find a ___ ___ ne," Angie murmured. "I thought it'd b___ ___ in to live around snow. Maybe I can even learn to ski."

"That sounds like quite an adventure for a single girl," Rose noted. "I admire young women who aren't afraid to follow their dreams."

Angie nodded and looked out the window. *If she only knew how fearful I really am. I'm not following my dreams; I'm running from a mess.* She leaned back in her seat, closed her eyes, and pretended to sleep. She didn't want to have to explain her tumultuous life any further.

Sensing Angie's tension, Rose spent most of the trip preparing for her summer classes, while Angie dozed or stared blankly out the window. Having worked with young people all her adult life, she understood the need for quiet contemplation during troubled times.

At long last a faint speck of Oahu came into view and gradually became larger and larger. All the passengers leaned toward the windows as the details of the island began to take shape. "To the right is the famous Punchbowl Memorial Cemetery," Rose said as she pointed to a dome-shaped structure on a grassy knoll. "Many of our war heroes are buried there."

The plane bounced onto the runway and taxied toward the terminal. "We have a two-hour layover before our plane leaves for Seattle. I know of a real cute restaurant not far from the gate we'll be leaving from. Let me treat you to dinner."

"Okay . . . sure," Angie smiled. "That's very generous of you."

The excitement of the landing, disembarking, and the hustle and bustle of the terminal distracted Angie from her inner turmoil. Even though Guam was becoming a melting pot of races, until she met Jay, she had stayed primarily with her own Chamorro people. The Honolulu airport was filled with nearly every nationality on earth. Some were dressed in eastern garb, others in western wear, and many in island wear. Tour groups from Japan and the mainland were greeted

by hostesses with a lei for each of the vaca-
tioners.

The two-hour layover passed quickly as
the two acquaintances browsed the gift
shops and dined in a Chinese restaurant.
The college professor's enthusiasm for life
was contagious, and Angie's fears did not
resurface until she was on the plane again
heading for Seattle. She again tried to watch
another boring movie and sleep, but her
fears consumed her. *I wonder if the people of
Rocky Bluff will like me, especially Jay's family. What if I can't get used to the cold
weather? What if I'm not able to earn enough
to support myself?* Angie's thoughts became
consumed with "what ifs," and she fought
to choke back her tears.

When the Hawaiian airliner landed in
Seattle, Rose walked her to the gate where
the Northwest flight to Great Falls would
depart. They arrived just as the other passengers were beginning to board. Angie hurriedly thanked Rose for her help and presented her boarding pass to the agent at the
door. She silently thanked God for giving
her Rose to guide her through the crowded
terminals. More than ever before, Angie's
frightening world closed in around her. She
surveyed the male passengers on the plane.
Are any of them capable of rape? she pon-

dered. The better groomed they were the more frightened she became of them.

The drive from Rocky Bluff to Great Falls was uneventful for Rebecca Hatfield and Edith Dutton. The bright red harvesters provided a vivid contrast to the fields of ripened wheat surrounding the highway. The last days of summer always provided a flurry of activities in Montana. Rebecca and Edith discussed the sights and events they'd like to share with their new guest. If there was time the next morning, they hoped to visit the Charlie Russell Museum and Art Gallery, then Giant Springs Park before leaving Great Falls. With the young people's luncheon, the Sunday buffet, and the Little Big Horn County Fair the next week, there was a myriad of events to enjoy. There was always something new and exciting to do in the Treasure State.

Upon arriving in Great Falls, Rebecca and Edith checked into the Holiday Inn. They enjoyed a relaxing dinner in the hotel dining room, then headed for the Great Falls International Airport an hour before Angie's plane was scheduled to arrive. Both were beside themselves with anticipation. Rebecca would again have a link to her beloved Guam, while Edith hoped for another link to her beloved grandson.

Rebecca mechanically stopped her car at the red light at the corner of Tenth Avenue South and Fifteenth Street. *Great Falls has got to be one of the most orderly cities in the country,* she thought as she patiently waited for the light to change. She was halfway across the intersection after the light turned green when she screamed.

A red pickup truck coming from the right slammed into the rear panel of her Chrysler Fifth Avenue. "Dear Jesus, help us," Edith gasped as the car spun around and blocked traffic in both directions.

When the car finally jerked to a stop, Rebecca looked over at her friend. "Are you okay?"

"I think so," Edith gasped. "I'm just thankful to still be alive."

The next hour was a blur of events. Rebecca and the driver of the pick-up were able to move their vehicles to the side street, away from the flow of traffic. The Great Falls police were on the scene within minutes. Rebecca was prepared for the usual presenting of driver's licenses and insurance companies; much to her chagrin the other driver was uninsured. The police did not waste time before writing tickets for speeding, failure to stop at a red light, and failure to have proper insurance. The young man dressed in a cowboy hat and boots did his best to soften his role in the mishap, but to no avail. The police were more determined than ever to charge him with the traffic violations.

In the background a wail of sirens drew closer. An ambulance pulled to a stop behind Rebecca's car, and two attendants jumped out. "Is anyone hurt?" the driver asked as he hurried toward the officer.

"Check the passenger in the car," he replied as he nodded toward Edith who had her head laid back on the seat, relaxing. "I understand that she has a heart condition."

The two emergency medical technicians hurried to the side of the car and opened the car. "Are you all right, Ma'am?"

"I think I'm just shaken a little," Edith replied cautiously.

"Let me check your pulse and blood pressure," the paramedic continued as he reached into his bag for a stethoscope. Within minutes he was recording the data on his sheet.

"How is it?" she asked.

"Both your pulse and blood pressure are high, but not unreasonable for someone who has just been in a car accident. I'd suggest you go home and relax. If you have any problems, be sure and get in touch with your family physician right away."

"I'm from Rocky Bluff," Edith explained. "We're on our way to the airport to pick up my grandson's friend." She glanced nervously at her watch. "In fact, the plane would have landed fifteen minutes ago."

Edith fidgeted, while Rebecca finished talking with the police. Her eyes scanned the skies for incoming flights. Much to her chagrin, lights were rising skyward from the bluff on which the airport was located. With so few planes in and out of the Great Falls airport, it was obvious that this was Angie's plane departing.

Rebecca took a deep breath as she slid behind the wheel of her damaged car. "I hope Angie doesn't arrive before we get there. Can you imagine how frightening it would be to be in a strange place, not knowing a soul and not knowing what to do?"

"I think she's already there," Edith sighed as the car turned back onto Tenth Avenue South and headed for the airport. "It looked like her plane taking off a few minutes ago."

Rebecca stopped her car in the ten-minute parking area. Only airport personnel were in the nearly vacant terminal. She wanted to run up the escalator to find her young friend, but she knew Edith was not capable of keeping up with her. The pair hurried through security and went to the desolate gate where the plane from Seattle landed. An attendant at a nearby gate confirmed their worst fear. That plane had landed more than a half hour before.

Rebecca and Edith next headed toward the baggage claim area. There in a corner sat a frightened Pacific Island girl surrounded by suitcases, sobbing hysterically. The look of terror in her eyes cut deep into Edith's and Rebecca's hearts. The last half hour must have been one of the longest in her short lifetime. It would take a major miracle to restore that broken spirit, but did they have the capacity to reach into the inner crevices of her soul?

CHAPTER 8

"Angie," Rebecca shouted as she ran toward the sobbing young woman.

Angie collapsed into Rebecca's arms and continued sobbing as the older woman embraced her. "You came," Angie choked. "I thought you didn't want me to come and weren't able to get ahold of me."

"Oh, Angie, we're excited about you coming. Please forgive me for being late. It must have been terrible for you. We had an accident an hour ago, and I couldn't get away."

"I'm sorry. I couldn't imagine that you would let me down, but I was so scared," Angie replied as she reached for a tissue to dry her eyes.

"Angie, I'd like you to meet Jay's grandmother, Edith Dutton. Edith, this is Angie Quinata."

Edith stepped forward and hugged Angie as if she were an old friend. "Welcome to Montana. I'm so happy to meet you at last.

Jay has told me so much about you in his letters."

"Edith, it's so nice to finally meet you. Jay told me you were praying for us daily. It's been so terrible, I don't know what I'd have done without knowing I had prayer support from all parts of the world."

Rebecca surveyed the desolate terminal. "I don't see anyone to help us with the baggage, but there's a row of carts down the way. I'm parked in the loading zone so I'm sure we can handle them ourselves."

Edith followed as Rebecca and Angie loaded the cart and headed for the Hatfields' Chrysler. Much to Rebecca's dismay the trunk was too bent to open. She tried to open the back door, but it too was bent and would not budge. With frustration, Rebecca pushed the cart to the left side of the car and began loading Angie's luggage. "I'm sorry, but it looks like you'll have to ride in front with us," Rebecca noted. "I can't make enough room back in the backseat."

"That's okay. I just hope I don't crowd the two of you," Angie replied timidly.

"That's one advantage of larger cars," Rebecca chuckled as she motioned for Angie to slide into the middle of the seat. "Space is no problem."

Angie's eyes danced as she saw the lights of the city spread for miles as Rebecca turned onto I-15 from the Great Falls airport. On Guam the island is so flat and the vegetation so thick that drivers can only see for a few yards at any given point. As Angie began to relax in the warmth and friendship of Rebecca and Edith, fatigue overtook her. "What time is it here?"

"Ten o'clock," Edith replied.

"It seems strange to have spent more than eighteen hours in the air or in terminals, and it's only four hours later than when I left."

"Our bodies get so confused when we cross the International Date Line," Rebecca agreed. "It usually took me at least three days to get over my jet lag when I flew back and forth from Guam."

"Now I understand why Guam is known as 'Where America's Day Begins'," Angie laughed as she laid her head against the seat.

"Are you hungry?" Edith queried. "It's probably been quite awhile since you ate."

"I'm sorry, but I'm just too tired to sit in a restaurant," Angie sighed. "I could take a nap in the car if you want to stop."

Rebecca glanced at her young friend in her rearview window. "We'll do nothing of the sort," she scolded gently. "We'll call room service when we get back to the hotel."

"I think I'm too tired to even eat, but it's been awhile so I suppose I should before I fall asleep," Angie replied as she closed her eyes in exhaustion.

Arriving at the hotel, Rebecca parked her car near the doorway closest to their room. She turned off the engine and slid from behind the wheel. "Angie, what suitcases will you need for the night?"

Angie followed Edith out the passenger side door. "Everything I need is in my shoulder bag."

"Good, it's right on top," Rebecca replied as she took the bag from the backseat.

As soon as Angie saw the bed, she collapsed lengthwise across it. It seemed like forever since she had slept in a bed. "I could use a small bowl of rice and a glass of milk before I go to sleep."

Edith and Rebecca exchanged glances. "Sorry," Edith replied. "Rice isn't on the hotel menu. Montana is beef and potatoes country. Would you like to see the menu?"

Angie glanced through the menu. "I guess I'll have a lot to get used to . . . a club sandwich with a soda will be fine."

Edith and Rebecca also decided on sandwiches and pop. While Rebecca was on the phone to room service, Edith looked over at Angie who was sobbing softly into the pillow. Edith sat on the bed beside her. "What's wrong, Dear?"

Angie turned her face toward her new friend. "I can't explain it," she sobbed. "It's just too much. Everything is happening too fast, and I'm so confused."

"I know it's hard having gone through the most traumatic experience in your life and now to be halfway around the world," Edith said softly as she brushed Angie's dark hair away from her eyes. "When my husband was in a nursing home, one of the nurses taught me how to give a back massage to help him relax before going to sleep. I may be a little rusty, but would you like a massage?"

"It sounds great," Angie replied. "The muscles in my neck and shoulders feel like they're tied in knots."

While Edith massaged Angie's tight muscles, she shared some of the antics of Jay's growing-up years and how he used to play airplane pilot with his friend, Ryan Reynolds. The bond between the two was instantaneous and based on something deeper than their common love for Jay Harkness. There seemed to be more healing in Edith's hands than the mere massaging of sore muscles.

"Angie, Sunday afternoon I'm planning a welcoming brunch for you to give you a chance to meet all the Harkness clan and many of our close friends."

"How thoughtful," Angie replied.

"Saturday, if it's all right with you, I've invited Dawn, Jay's sister, and some of her friends for pizza and a video. I thought it would be nice if you got to meet some of the young people of Rocky Bluff."

"That is very kind of you," Angie yawned.

While Edith massaged Angie's back and neck, Rebecca called Andy to tell him about the accident. She didn't want to shock him when she drove into the drive with a damaged car.

When their sandwiches arrived, Angie quietly ate, then prepared for bed. Within minutes she was fast asleep. A look of peaceful relaxation covered the young girl's face as she lay sleeping in a hotel half the world away from her home. Instead of leaving everyone she loved behind, she again was immersed in love and acceptance.

Angie's arrival in Rocky Bluff was not fully understood and supported by the younger generation. Rumors abounded as to the nature of the Pacific Islander.

"Mom, do I have to take my friends over

to Grandma's Saturday?" Dawn Harkness protested. "It'll be embarrassing explaining to them that my brother, the most handsome guy in his graduating class, fell in love with a foreigner."

Nancy Harkness looked at her daughter and shook her head with disbelief. "Dawn, I'm surprised that you feel that way. Guamanians are American citizens the same as you are. Their culture may be slightly different from yours, but so what? You've lived around Native Americans all your life, and some have become your close friends. Please give Angie a chance. Your grandmother would be heartbroken if she heard you say that."

Dawn hung her head. "I suppose. I don't want to hurt Grandma's feelings." Dawn then forced a smile. "Besides, Jay will be furious with me if I don't treat his girlfriend right. I'll talk to the girls about what video to get, and we can order a couple pizzas to go with it. I know Sarah's going to be hurt meeting Angie. Ever since she was in junior high, she's had a crush on Jay. After all, he and Ryan were the stars of both the football and the basketball teams."

"I knew I could depend on you," Nancy replied. "Just remember what you would feel like if what happened to Angie had happened to you. Think how scared she must feel never having been off the island of Guam before and suddenly to be in the wide open spaces of Montana. She needs all the love and support the people of Rocky Bluff can give her. Being sized up by a bunch of critical teens will only make it harder for her."

Dawn was proud of her brother, but as she grew into her teens, she felt more and more pushed into the background as her teachers, fellow students, and the community members compared her with her brother's athletic ability. The comparison didn't hold up. Dawn excelled in music and could care less about sports.

Several of her friends were looking forward to Jay returning to Rocky Bluff after his discharge from the Air Force. Now Jay was sending a Chamorro girl to Rocky Bluff ahead of him. Even though he claimed they were not engaged, that was the only conclusion Dawn's friends could make. The most eligible guy in town was now taken by an outsider.

Edith Dutton and Rebecca Hatfield awoke around seven o'clock. They bathed and dressed, while Angie's sleep was so deep that she scarcely moved the entire night. The older women curled up with favorite

154

books to avoid waking the weary traveler. By eight-thirty Rebecca whispered, "Edith, we're going to be needing breakfast pretty soon, but I'd hate to awaken Angie. Let's call room service for breakfast. We don't have to check out until eleven."

"Sounds good. I am getting a little hungry," Edith agreed. "Let me take another look at their room service menu."

"I'll load our luggage in the car while we wait for room service," Rebecca whispered as she finished closing her suitcase.

The rest of the morning, Rebecca and Edith quietly enjoyed their breakfast, then propped themselves on their beds and enjoyed their leisure reading. Every few minutes they glanced at the beautiful young girl peacefully sleeping in the next bed. At ten-thirty Edith became concerned. "If we have to be out of here by eleven, don't you think we ought to wake Angie so she has time to get ready?"

"I hate to do so, but we really don't have a choice," Rebecca replied. "Maybe we'll have a little time to stop at the mall before we head back to Rocky Buff."

Edith bent over Angie's bed and shook her shoulder gently. "Angie, Angie. I hate to wake you, but we're going to have to check out in a few minutes."

Angie's muscles tightened as she sat up with a start. A shrill scream filled the room. A look of terror was in her eyes.

"Angie, it's okay," Edith assured her as she stroked her shoulder. "You're in Montana with friends."

The young woman rubbed her eyes and looked around the room. "I'm sorry. I don't know why I wake up screaming. It's happened a lot to me lately."

"You're probably suffering from Post Traumatic Stress Syndrome," Edith explained as Angie gradually stopped trembling. "It's a very common malady. Hopefully, it will go away as you become more secure in your new environment."

"Before we leave town, would you like to stop at the mall and find some winter clothes?" Edith asked as Angie reached for her robe.

"I don't think I'll have enough money to do any serious shopping until after I've worked for a few weeks," Angie replied meekly.

"I'd like to help you with that," Edith replied. "I received a little extra money from Roy's life insurance policy, and I'm certain helping you get reestablished would be exactly what he would have chosen himself."

"But I've never worn winter clothes before. I don't know what to look for."

"We'll help you," Rebecca inserted. "All you'll need to do is tell us which style out of many you like the best."

"But this is August. Do they have coats in the stores now?"

"The back-to-school sales are starting, and they always have a good supply of winter wear then. It should be a lot of fun." Edith smiled.

The remainder of the day was a blur of activities for Angie. First there was lunch in the mall restaurant, then there was the flurry of trying on clothes — a lightweight jacket, then a heavy winter coat, a scarf, gloves, boots, three sweaters, dress slacks, jeans, and a couple of wool suits. At the cash register, Angie was afraid to look at the total as Edith reached for her credit card. *Why would someone I just met yesterday be willing to do all this for me?* Angie asked herself.

The clerk helped the women load their parcels into a shopping cart. "Thank you," Edith said. "You've been most helpful."

Rebecca pushed the cart to her Chrysler and unloaded the packages in the backseat on top of Angie's suitcases. The wind tossed their hair in all directions. "This is the kind of wind we get on Guam before a typhoon," Angie said matter-of-factly.

"Great Falls is one of the windiest cities in the United States," Rebecca chuckled, "but the natives are used to it. They go about their business without even noticing it."

As Rebecca headed east toward the city limits, Angie marveled at Highwood Mountains to the left and the Little Belt Mountains in the far distant right. "The mountains are more beautiful in real life than in any picture or TV program. There's such a sense of peace and tranquillity about them."

"I know," Edith replied. "When Roy and I were able to drive, after we'd have a particularly frustrating day, we'd get in the car and drive into the mountains. We had a special spot where we liked to park and sit on a log and gaze at the vast plains below. Somehow that seemed to make our problems seem so small."

Angie smiled as she responded eagerly to her friend. "I hope you'll show me that spot. I love to meditate in peaceful surroundings."

"I'm sure we can find someone to drive us there. It's the most beautiful sight at sunset," Edith promised.

The three women rode in silence for several miles. Angie's eyes sparkled as she surveyed the rolling fields of golden wheat with harvesters busy at work. Never before had she been able to see for scores of miles at a time. Her gaze then drifted to the dashboard . . . sixty-five miles per hour. . . . "I've never been in a car going this fast," she giggled. "The roads are so crowded on Guam that the speed limit is thirty-five miles per hour."

Before long, fatigue again overtook Angie. She laid her head back on the seat and closed her eyes. It was completely dark when Rebecca stopped in front of Edith Dutton's home. Rebecca retrieved Edith's overnight bag from the backseat and carried it to Edith's front door. "Thanks for riding with me," Rebecca said as she set the suitcase inside the front door. "I'll be sure that Angie has a ride to your house Saturday noon; then I'll see you Sunday at her welcoming buffet."

Angie was just awakening as Rebecca returned to her car. "Edith has a nice home. I'm looking forward to having lunch there Saturday."

"Jay's sister, Dawn, and some of her friends are going to be there as well. I hope you like pizza."

"I love it. I hope Dawn is like her brother."

"I'm sure you'll enjoy yourself," Rebecca replied as she parked her car in her driveway on Rimrock Road. Andy soon appeared at the front door. He greeted Angie and Rebecca warmly and began carrying Angie's bags to her basement suite. Within half an hour, Angie was again fast asleep in bed. The combination of emotional and physical exhaustion had taken its toll on her petite body.

The next day, Angie had a leisurely breakfast with Rebecca and Andy. She was immediately impressed with Andy's devotion to his new bride. For someone who had lived the confirmed bachelor lifestyle for nearly all his adult life, Andy seemed to have a sensitivity of how two shall become one. *I wish I could someday have the kind of marriage the Hatfields have, but after what has happened, I'll never be able to be a pure, true bride.*

Later Rebecca took Angie sightseeing. She drove the streets of Rocky Bluff and pointed out historic landmarks. Everything seemed new and strange to Angie. She pictured Jay as a young boy riding his bicycle down the wide, tree-lined streets. No wonder he never stopped talking about his home in Montana, she thought.

Rebecca turned off Main Street and parked her car in front of the Looking Glass Salon. "This is where you're going to be working. I want you to meet Barbara Old Tail. I'm sure you'll like her. She's very proud of her Native American ancestry and has just moved her mother from the reservation to live with her."

Barb was polishing the mirrors in the new addition to her salon when Rebecca and Angie entered. After Rebecca did the formal introduction, Barb and Angie began speaking beauticians' talk as if they were old cosmetology school classmates. Rebecca was amazed at how the two were so well matched for each other. *Maybe Angie's adjustment to Rocky Bluff won't be so difficult after all,* she told herself.

CHAPTER 9

"Girls, I'll leave you alone to watch the video," Edith Dutton said. "I'm going to take a quick nap. Wake me when it's over. Besides, I've already read the book, and I don't want to spoil it with the movie," she chuckled.

Dawn, Angie, and Dawn's friends, Tara Wolf, Linda Wright, and Marsha Harris, made themselves comfortable in Edith's living room. Tara stretched out on the floor while Dawn, Linda, and Marsha curled up on the sofa, and Angie sat in a reclining chair.

"Angie, the name of the movie we selected is *A River Runs Through It,*" Dawn Harkness explained as she took the video out of the box. "It's getting kind of old, but it was filmed here in Montana, and I thought you might enjoy it."

Angie's eyes brightened as she leaned back in the recliner nearest the television. The chair had been Roy's favorite before he went to the nursing home. "That was kind of you. I've been fascinated by this state ever since I met Jay."

"Rumor has it that you and Jay are engaged. Are you planning to get married soon?" Marsha asked as she flipped her long blond hair over her shoulder.

"I don't know how that rumor ever got started." Angie grimaced. "I doubt if I'll ever marry."

"See, Marsha, there might still be hope for you after all," Dawn teased. "Jay'll be coming home for good in June. He'll be surprised that you're no longer a skinny high school freshman but a beautiful college coed."

"After I get to the university, I may not be interested in Jay anymore," Marsha retorted. "I'll have to size up all the fraternity guys before I make a decision."

The group howled with laughter as a look of confusion spread over Angie's face. She had never been in a group before where trapping a guy was treated as a game. Angie tried to ignore the conversation going on around her and became enthralled with the photography of the majestic mountains and the art of fly fishing. She had lived around deep-sea fishing all her life, and this was an entirely new concept to her. The others watched the video with polite boredom for awhile, but gradually their conversations became more animated. Angie tried to ignore the whispering going on around her and focused on the movie. Little by little she began to catch bits and fragments of their conversation.

"When are you leaving for college?". . . . "What party did you go to last week?". . . . "Who was there?". . . . "What were they drinking?". . . . "How much?". . . . "What were they smoking?". . . . "Who ended the night in a motel with whom?"

The beauty of the movie faded into the background as Angie became more and more troubled by the conversation going on around her. *Are all stateside teenagers like this? Jay would be shocked if he knew his sister ran with such a crowd. After being associated with what went on at Coiffures and Manicures, I don't want to have anything to do with these girls, but Jay will be crushed if I don't make friends with his sister.*

Toward the end of the video, Edith returned to the living room. "How's the movie?"

"Fascinating," Angie replied. "I hope someday I'll be able to see some of those places it showed."

"I'm sure someone will be able to take you to western Montana. It's totally different from the central and eastern part of the state," Edith said.

Within minutes, the credits began to roll, and Dawn stood to turn off the recorder. "I have some things I need to get done this afternoon. Angie, would you like me to drop you off at Rebecca's on the way?"

"I'd appreciate that," Angie replied, then turned her attention back to Edith. "I want to thank you for lunch and for a pleasant afternoon."

"I'm glad you could come," the older woman replied. "I'm looking forward to introducing you to the rest of the family tomorrow at the buffet."

Angie nodded in agreement and followed the others to Dawn's car. All five of them crowded into the small vehicle, and Dawn sped toward Rimrock Road. Everyone in the car appeared happy and carefree except Angie. The cloud of alienation and frustration hung heavy over her. *Why did I ever come to Montana? I just don't fit in.*

Rebecca was bursting with news when Angie walked in the front door. "Welcome back," she greeted. "How was your afternoon?"

"The video was great. They played *A River*

Runs Through It, and the scenery was beautiful."

"I dearly loved that video and watched it three times," Rebecca replied. "You received a phone call while you were gone."

"Who was it?"

"Jay. He said he'd call back tomorrow evening."

Angie spent the remainder of the day relaxing. Life in Rocky Bluff was so different from Guam. Rebecca, Edith, and Barb Old Tail had accepted her with warmth and understanding, but the younger people seemed to keep her at a distance.

The next morning, Angie attended church with Rebecca and Andy. She enjoyed the music, and Pastor Rhodes's sermon about forgiveness and salvation through Jesus Christ was like salve on the open sore of her heart. *If only I could keep this feeling forever,* Angie thought as she sang the closing hymn.

As Angie followed Rebecca down the side aisle, an attractive, middle-aged woman approached her. "Hi, you must be Angie Quinata," she greeted. "My name is Teresa Lennon. Welcome to Rocky Bluff. I'm so glad you could come and help Barb Old Tail in her salon."

"It's nice to meet you, Mrs. Lennon," Angie replied. "I'm looking forward to working with Barb. It was nice of her to offer me a job when I was halfway around the world."

"Please call me Teresa," she insisted. "I'm sure we'll be seeing a lot of each other during the next few months. In fact, I was planning to attend your welcome-to-Montana buffet at Edith's this afternoon."

Angie was impressed with the warmth Teresa had for her even though they had never met. When she joined her host family in the parking lot, she couldn't help but ask, "Rebecca, tell me about Teresa Lennon. She's especially sweet and understanding."

"She's had lots of experience dealing with women who have been traumatized," Rebecca explained. "She's the director of the Spouse Abuse Center. She's dealt with all kinds of domestic and violent situations."

"Has she ever dealt with rape victims?" Angie queried.

"I can't say for sure, but as far as I know, there's never been a rape in Rocky Bluff."

Angie's eyes fell to the ground as a faint smile spread across her face. *What a lucky place,* she thought.

Andy opened the doors of the newly-repaired Chrysler for the women.

"We have time to go home and take a quick nap before we go to Edith's. You'll need all the rest you can get," Andy chuckled. "The Harkness clan is a mighty big family to meet all at once."

"I am a little nervous," Angie admitted, "but I did promise Edith I'd be there."

"She's a perfect hostess. You'll feel right at home," Rebecca assured her.

Two hours later, the Hatfields and Angie arrived at Edith's home. Edith welcomed them with a warm hug. A dark-haired, distinguished-looking couple emerged from the kitchen. "Angie, I'd like you to meet Jay's parents, Nancy and Bob Harkness."

Angie extended her right hand to greet them, but Nancy embraced her. "Angie, we've heard so much about you. I feel like I've known you all my life."

"Thank you," Angie murmured. "You have a very nice son."

Bob took Angie's hand in both of his. "Welcome to Rocky Bluff. I hope you'll come to love the community as much as we do."

Before Angie could respond, the doorbell rang, and Edith hurried to answer it. An athletic young man of Angie's own age entered the room. Finally, Edith turned back to the guest of honor. "Angie, I'd like you to meet Ryan Reynolds. He's

Jay's closest friend. He's now attending Montana A&M in Butte. Ryan, this is Angie Quinata."

Ryan extended his right hand. "It's nice meeting you, Angie."

Angie flushed under her copper skin. "Hi, Ryan. Jay has told me a lot about you and of your love of sports."

"Good for him," Ryan laughed. His laugh was infectious, and soon Jay's parents and grandmother were caught up in the conversation about incidents Ryan and Jay had shared from Little League baseball through high school.

The talk flew happily and freely as Angie's reservations about Dawn subsided. Within minutes, Jay's aunt and uncle, Jean and Jim Thompson, and their two little girls arrived from Running Butte. Close behind came Ryan's older brother, Larry, his wife, Libby, and their two children.

Bob Harkness took some folding chairs out of the closet for the additional guests. The doorbell rang again, and Teresa Lennon greeted Angie. Then Pastor Rhodes and his wife, Thelma, arrived, and Dawn came with Marsha and Tara. The doorbell kept ringing, and guest after guest filled the living room, dining area, and kitchen. Edith's home echoed with love and laughter. *No wonder Jay loves Rocky Bluff and can hardly wait to return,* Angie sighed.

Angie's eyes often drifted to the corner where the three teenage girls sat, immersed in their own conversation of how soon they would be leaving Rocky Bluff and going to college. *What is it that concerns me so much about them?* she asked herself. *They act like Rocky Bluff is the last place on earth they want to be, and yet Dawn has such a delightful family.*

Everyone filled their plates from the abundance of food loaded on the dining room table and the nearby counters and scattered throughout the house and backyard. Even though laughter and warmth echoed throughout the crowd, Angie was overwhelmed by the sea of faces. She had always been comfortable with two or three people at a time, but this loud and friendly crowd was so foreign to her. She withdrew from it more and more and finally sat on the corner of the patio by herself. Visions of tropical palm trees replaced the pine trees in Edith Dutton's backyard. Instead of Edith, Rebecca, Teresa, or Nancy, she was seeing her mother's face. Tears filled her eyes, and she choked back a sob.

"All these people getting too much for you?" Edith whispered as she put her arm around Angie and sat on the step beside her.

"I was just thinking about home and the people there," Angie admitted. "I guess I'm not used to being the center of attention."

The late summer sun glistened off Edith's silver-gray hair. "I felt much the same way when my first husband introduced his family to me here in Rocky Bluff. They were a bunch who worked hard, played hard, and laughed easily, but I would rather have curled up quietly in a corner with a good book. However, through the years I've become a lot like them."

"You have a wonderful family," Angie replied. "Now I understand why Jay is so much fun to be with."

"You've been such a good sport putting up with all of us," Edith said. "Would you like to go back to Rebecca's now?"

Angie nodded as she looked up and smiled into Edith's warm, affirming face. In only a few words, Jay's grandmother was able to articulate the feelings stirring within her.

"I'll go get Rebecca, and you can slip out the side, if you'd like. I'll explain to everyone that you're tired and still suffering from jet lag and need to get some rest."

Angie could not refrain from embracing Edith. "Thank you for your understanding.

You have a wonderful family, and I'm look-ing forward to getting to know each one of them individually, but I'm just brain-dead today."

"Don't try to explain. Everyone will understand," Edith said as she stood to find Rebecca and Andy.

Within minutes, Angie was relaxing with one of Andy's Western novels in the solitude of her sitting room in Rebecca's basement. She had never been interested in Western novels or movies before, but now that she had seen Montana, she could relate to the vastness of the land and the frontier spirit of its people. She was lost in the world of frontier life when a shout echoed down the steps. "Angie, Jay's on the telephone."

Angie raced up the stairs and grabbed the phone lying on the counter. "Hello," she panted.

"Angie, how are you?" Jay greeted, excited to finally hear her familiar voice.

"I'm fine," Angie assured him. "I'm begin-ning to get over my jet lag. How are you doing?"

"Guam isn't the same without you," Jay replied. "I've already started my planning calendar until June when I'll be able to come back to Rocky Bluff. Every evening I mark off another day."

"June seems so far away. I can't even think past next week."

"What all's happening? Rebecca said you met my entire family this afternoon."

"Your grandmother went to a lot of work to throw a welcoming buffet for me, but I made such a fool out of myself."

Jay burst into his infectious laugh. "What could you have possibly done to make a fool out of yourself?"

"Jay, it's not funny," Angie protested. "Everyone was being so kind to me; then I got homesick for Guam and started crying. Rebecca and Andy had to bring me home."

"I'll admit my family can become overly exuberant and overwhelming at times."

"They were absolutely delightful," Angie retorted. "I'm used to small, relaxed groups and occasionally some fussing from relatives. Your family genuinely enjoys being with one another. I can understand why you're so anxious to get back and see everyone."

"How was Dawn?" Jay queried.

Angie gulped. She didn't want to hide anything from Jay, but she didn't want to cause hard feelings in the family. "Your grandmother invited her and some of her friends for pizza and videos yesterday."

"So how was Dawn doing?" Jay persisted.

"I liked Dawn a lot."

"She is a sweet girl," Jay continued, "but she's not writing anymore, and she's never home when I call."

"She's busy working and getting ready to go to college. She's planning to join a sorority as soon as she gets there. I think she already has one picked out. I met a friend of hers who's trying to get Dawn to join her sorority."

"Do you remember the name of that friend?"

"Tara Wolf, I think."

There was a long pause on the line. "Oh no, not Tara. She's one of the biggest party girls that Rocky Bluff has produced in recent years. I've heard rumors that her sorority is one of the wildest on campus. I hope Dawn doesn't get involved with them."

"I'm sorry I told you something to concern you. Maybe it won't be as bad as you think."

"I hope not," Jay sighed. "At least Dawn has had a good upbringing, and underneath everything she knows right from wrong."

"I'm sure she'll get direction to her life soon," Angie tried to assure him. "She has such a sweet personality underneath all that frivolous facade."

"Thanks," Jay replied. "I needed to hear

that. Now let's get back to you. When do you start work?"

"I officially start the first of September. I hope my box of beauty supplies gets here by then."

"Didn't you take them with you?"

"No. I was over the luggage limit so Mother had to mail them to me. Hopefully, they'll be here next week; otherwise I won't be able to start."

"If it doesn't arrive on time, it will give you a few more days to see Montana."

"The county fair is next week, and Rebecca and some of her friends want me to go. There's a rodeo at night which I'm really excited about seeing. I've never seen anything like that before."

"It's good to see a rodeo at least once," Jay replied, "but prepare yourself. Sometimes the crowd can become extremely rowdy."

Tears began to build in Angie's eyes. "How's Mother?"

"I'm sorry, I've been awfully busy at work. I haven't seen her since we left the airport. I'll try to give her a call when I get off the phone and let her know you are doing well."

Angie's tears turned to sobs. "Please tell Mom that I love her and I miss her very much."

CHAPTER 10

Angie Quinata unpacked her beauty supplies in her station at the Looking Glass Beauty Salon in Rocky Bluff, Montana, one week later than expected. She checked the post office every day until the parcel from Guam finally arrived. Rebecca drove Angie home with her treasured box. Angie hurried inside and reached for the phone book. She dialed the number and waited.

"Looking Glass Beauty Salon," Barbara Old Tail greeted.

"Hello, Barbara. This is Angie. My supplies from Guam finally arrived."

"Great. When would you like to begin work?"

"Right away," Angie replied eagerly.

"Would you be able to come to the salon now so I can run home and check on Mother?"

"I'd be glad to. See you in fifteen minutes."

Angie's heart pounded as Rebecca drove her downtown. After three months of confusion, she was finally having an opportunity to start over in the profession she loved. Six weeks ago she was sure all her hard work at Guam Community College had been in vain.

Angie was all smiles as she walked into the Looking Glass Salon. The shop sparkled with cleanliness, and the decor was simple, warm, and homey, much different from the plush interior of Coiffure and Manicure in Agana, Guam.

"Welcome," Barb greeted. "You came at a good time. It's been kind of quiet this morning so I'll have time to show you around."

She motioned for Angie to follow her. "This station will be yours. Set your box here."

"You've decorated this beautifully," Angie noted.

"Rebecca helped me with the remodeling. You wouldn't believe how small this was before."

"I must say you both have good taste," Angie said as she surveyed the mauve-flowered wallpaper trim.

"Thank you," Barb replied as she led the way to the back room. "This is nothing fancy. Just the usual washer and dryer, supply cabinets, microwave, refrigerator, and chairs." Barb laughed as she pointed to the side wall. "My next project is to replace that old sofa."

"It looks comfortable," Angie replied as she observed the threadbare green couch.

"It is," Barb chuckled. "That's why I've never wanted to part with it. Maybe I'll just have it reupholstered instead."

Barb led Angie back to the front counter. "This is our schedule book. We'll just divide the columns in half; yours on the right and mine on the left. My home number is in the automatic dial on the phone in case you have any questions."

"Thanks." Angie smiled. "Don't worry about a thing. I hope your mother is doing okay."

"She just gets lonely and confused if someone's not around. I never know what to expect from one minute to the next. I won't be gone long."

Barb reached for her sweater and hurried into the brisk fall breeze. Angie turned her attention back to her cherished box and her station. She painstakingly arranged and rearranged her curlers, curling irons, and bottles. *This area is not as large as what I had at Coiffure and Manicure, but the layout is much better,* Angie told herself.

Angie turned on the radio on the front counter. Country western music filled the salon. She spun the dial . . . more country western music. She moved the dial another notch . . . still more country western music. *You always know you're in the real West when that's all you can find on the radio,* she chuckled.

Angie's amusement was interrupted by the ringing of the phone. "Looking Glass Beauty Salon."

"Hello, Barbara?" the voice greeted.

"I'm sorry, but Barb is out of the salon now. This is Angie Quinata; I just started as her assistant. Is there anything I can help you with?"

"Well, hi, Angie. This is Teresa Lennon. I met you at church, then at Edith Dutton's house right after you arrived in Rocky Bluff."

"Oh yes, I remember you," Angie replied. "You're the director of the Spouse Abuse Center."

"That's right . . . and that's part of my problem. I just found out I have state inspectors coming from Helena in the morning, and my hair is a mess. Do you think you'd have time to give me a perm this afternoon?"

"Just set your time. You'll be my first

Rocky Bluff customer."

That afternoon as Angie rolled Teresa's hair, the young beautician was fascinated by the services the Spouse Abuse Center provided. "That sounds like such a worthwhile program," Angie noted. "I heard of several cases of spouse abuse on Guam, but if they didn't have family to turn to, they were just out of luck. If Guam had a Spouse Abuse Center, I wasn't aware of it."

"Emergency social services vary from location to location. Rocky Bluff is fortunate to have both a Crisis Line and a Spouse Abuse Center. They both work closely with each other and with the police department. For a community of this size to have both speaks well of the people here."

"In the two and a half weeks I've been here, I can't believe the personal support I've gotten," Angie said as she squeezed the curling solution into each roll of hair. "Not to be prying, but what happened to some of the women who've used your services? Were they able to get on their feet again?"

"We have a track record to be proud of," Teresa replied. "One of our clients went to the local community college for training, then became a successful paralegal. In the meantime, her husband was able to get his life straightened out, and they were later reconciled. A couple of other women who had suffered abuse became volunteers at the center during their transition period and later began a successful day care center. The list can go on and on. I'm pleased with each one of them."

As Angie rinsed the solution out of her customer's hair, her mind raced. *Outside of Rebecca and Edith I've never told anyone in Rocky Bluff about my attack. I wonder if they'd accept me if they knew the real reason why I came to Rocky Bluff.*

"Do you have a psychiatrist who works with the abused women?" Angie asked cautiously.

"I have a master's degree in psychology, and I counsel both individuals and small groups."

"Do you ever counsel women who have not suffered spousal abuse?"

Teresa studied Angie's face and body language. It was obvious she was trying to communicate something much deeper than her words. "Occasionally. Adjusting to a new environment can be extremely difficult, but a beauty shop is not a place to discuss personal matters. Can you come to the center Thursday morning?"

Angie's eyes brightened. "Thank you. My doctor suggested I seek counseling on

Guam, but I was afraid to go. I heard that some psychiatrists made fun of Christianity, and I needed someone who'd understand how important my faith is to me. I don't know how I'd get through tough times without looking to God for strength."

Just then Barb Old Tail returned. A smile spread across her face as she saw Angie already working on a customer. "I'm sorry it took so long. Mother was having a real confusing time, and I just couldn't get away. I see I left the shop in good hands."

"She's doing a mighty fine job," Teresa replied. "Angie's definitely an answer to your prayers."

The next few days flew by for Angie. The relaxed, casual mood of the clients and her employer helped the tension lines fade from her forehead. When Thursday morning arrived, she awoke early, dressed, ate breakfast, and hurried to the Spouse Abuse Center. Teresa was waiting for her.

She led Angie into a comfortable sitting room. "You're not going to ask me to lie down while you sit at the desk?" Angie asked.

Teresa burst into gales of laughter. "You've been watching too much television. We're sitting here as equals. You have training as a beautician, and I have training as a counselor."

Angie blushed with embarrassment. "I'm sorry. I've never been to a counselor before. I just got started working here, so I don't have much money to pay for your services."

"If that's the case, then let's make a deal. . . . Your counseling sessions for a wash and set twice a month, and haircuts and perms as needed."

"That sounds like the old-fashioned barter system," Angie giggled, "but it's a great idea."

For the rest of the hour, Angie poured out her anger and guilt over being raped and violated. Feelings that she never knew existed came tumbling out. There was much more she wanted to say, but it was time to go to work. She scheduled another meeting, then nearly skipped to the Looking Glass. Maybe there was hope for her yet.

When Angie returned home after work that evening, Rebecca was bursting with excitement. "Angie, do you have plans for Saturday afternoon?"

"No, why?"

"An old friend of mine is returning to Rocky Bluff this weekend. She and her family will be staying with Edith, and she's invited us over for lunch. I'm sure you'll like them."

"Sounds like fun. I'll try to be more relaxed than I was the last time I was at Edith's."

"You had every reason in the world to be upset that day. We all deluged upon you at the same time," Rebecca apologized. "From now on only small groups at a time will be allowed."

"Don't worry about me. I'm beginning to get adjusted now," Angie said as she got a soft drink from the refrigerator. "What's your friend like?"

"Her name is Beth Blair. Her story is a testimony to Edith Dutton and the Crisis Center. She came to town as a scared, pregnant sixteen-year-old runaway and left town seven years later with an education, an upstanding husband, a growing family, and the desire to finish her college degree. She worked as a clerk in the Rocky Bluff High School library when I was the librarian there. She now wants to become a librarian herself."

"I'd love to meet her. I can't imagine a community doing that much for an outsider. On Guam we always looked out for our own, but off-island people were on their own."

On Saturday Angie immediately fell in love with Beth Blair, her husband, Dan, seven-year-old Jeffey, and baby Edith. Conversation in the group flew easily and lightly. Much of it centered around the Crisis Center in Missoula, Montana, that Dan was managing while Beth was finishing her degree at the university. Dan had directed the Rocky Bluff Crisis Center and had received most of his training from Roy Dutton, Edith's second husband. They reminisced about old times and how the entire community pulled together when Jeffey was kidnapped from the day care center by his biological father and taken to Canada.

Later in the afternoon, Angie joined Beth in the bedroom where she was nursing Edith. "Beth, you've been through so much, and yet you seem so happy," Angie began as she sat on the corner of the bed. "How did you do it?"

"I didn't do anything but live my life the best I could," Beth replied. "It was the grace of God, all these good people in Rocky Bluff, and, of course, Dan who made the difference. I tried to do everything on my own and was completely upset and frustrated. That's when I called the Crisis Center and met Edith. She taught me to rely on God's strength and the encouragement of others. I'd never have survived the kidnapping without the support I received from Edith and her family."

"But didn't people criticize you because you were pregnant out of wedlock?"

"A few did behind my back. In fact, I got one terrible letter from a stranger during Jeffey's kidnapping saying I wasn't fit to be a mother, but the people that mattered knew that Christ died for my sins as well as theirs. They did everything in their power to build me up and help me start a new life."

"What about Dan? Didn't he have reservations about marrying someone who wasn't a . . . virgin?"

"When I ran away from home, my parents made me feel so guilty; I was sure I was spoiled for life and no one would ever want to marry me, but the people of Rocky Bluff taught me about true love and forgiveness. Dan stood by me through good times and bad and kept reassuring me that he loved me for what I was today, not what I used to be."

Tears built in Angie's eyes, and she began sobbing. Beth creased her forehead as she put her hand on her new friend's shoulder. "Angie, what's wrong?"

Angie tried to choke back her tears. "That's where I am today. Jay Harkness and I were extremely close friends, and we were talking about getting married as soon as he got out of the service. I had vowed I was going to remain pure until my wedding night, even though a lot of my friends thought I was old-fashioned and ridiculous. On my last day of college, I was raped on my way to the parking lot. The one thing I was saving for my husband is gone. I feel I am spoiled for life and can never marry."

"Jay must still love you; otherwise he wouldn't have sent you here to be with his family and friends," Beth reminded her.

"Jay has been a jewel even when I've been cruel and unkind to him. He even kept coming to take care of me after I gave him his friendship ring back. I just don't understand why."

"Sometimes it seems like there are few good men left," Beth replied gently, "but Dan and Jay have the integrity and compassion to love someone for what they are inside, not what has happened to them. Hang on to Jay; he's a man worth having."

Angie took out a tissue and dried her eyes. "I'm finding that out. Meeting the people who shaped his life is beginning to change my mind about never marrying anyone. Rocky Bluff is a unique place."

"That it is," Beth agreed, "but there are kind, compassionate people wherever you go. You just have to know where to look for them."

Just then Jeffey ran into the room. "Mommy, can you come watch a video with us? Granny Edith picked out a real funny one."

Beth looked at Angie who nodded her head, then turned back to her son. "Sure, let's go," she said as she slid off the bed and motioned for Angie to follow.

The next few weeks Angie had her first experience with the changing of the seasons. The beauty of the foliage in the fall was exactly as Jay had described it, only better. On Saturdays she helped Andy rake and bag the leaves that had fallen or blown into their yard. The crispness in the air made her feel invigorated and alert. She was thankful Rebecca and Edith had taken her shopping for fall clothes before they left Great Falls the day after she arrived. She would have had no idea how to select functional winter clothing.

The first snowfall of the winter came early.

The day before Halloween, Angie stood at the front window of the Looking Glass Salon and watched with fascination as the large flakes drifted gently to the ground. She had waited for years to see snow, and now she was finding it even more beautiful than she had expected. Business in the salon was light that morning so she took a chair near the window and wrote her mother.

Dear Mom,

I'm sorry I've been so negligent in my writing. There have been so many people to meet and things to do I feel as if I'm living in a whirlwind. I've appreciated all our phone conversations and all your letters. Before I left Guam, you said you were going to start saving your pennies so you could come to Rocky Bluff for Christmas to see me and the snow.

The first snow is falling today, and words can't express its beauty and intrigue. I can hardly wait to learn to ski.

How is your penny jar coming? Will you be able to come for Christmas?

Love,
Angie

Barbara Old Tail finished the haircut on her last client and looked nervously out the window. "If you wouldn't mind tending the shop by yourself, I think I better run home and check on Mother. She often gets confused when something different happens. She used to love the snow, but I don't know how she'll react to it this time."

"I'd be glad to," Angie replied. "If no one calls or stops in, I'll just sit here and watch the snow fall."

A feeling of apprehension engulfed Barb as she drove home. She put the key in the lock and was surprised to see that it was already unlocked. *I was sure I locked this door before I left this morning,* she thought. She turned the knob and walked inside. "Mother . . . Mother, I'm home."

Only her own voice echoed throughout the house. She ran from room to room. . . . No one. She opened the back door and surveyed the yard. . . . No one. Barb went to the coat closet and flung the door open. Sure enough, her mother's winter coat was gone.

When she reopened the front door, even her own footprints were covered with snow. There was no hope in following her mother's tracks.

Dear God, she prayed. *Please help me find her. Let her be okay.* Barb ran back to her car and drove around the block. All she saw were people standing in their windows watching the snow fall. She hurried back home to see if her mother had returned. The house was empty. Again she rushed to her car and drove for several more blocks without results. Returning home for the third time, Barb began calling her neighbors. Either no one was home or they had not seen an older woman walking in the snow.

She took a deep breath and dialed 9-1-1.

"Emergency services."

"This is Barbara Old Tail. I'd like to report a missing person. She suffers from Alzheimer's, and I'm afraid she's in danger if she's wandering in this snow."

The dispatcher got a complete description of Barb's mother and the pattern of her behavior and assured her she would send as many police as possible to the streets to search for her.

Barb then called Edith Dutton. "Hello, Edith, this is Barb Old Tail. Are you still chairing the church prayer chain?" she queried as soon as the gray-haired matriarch of the church answered the phone.

"Yes, I am. Is something wrong?"

"Very. I came home from the salon to check on Mother, but she's wandered away.

I've driven through the neighborhood and called all the neighbors, and no one has seen her. I just asked the police to search for her. Would you ask the prayer chain to pray that we find her before she gets too cold?"

"How dreadful," Edith sighed. "We'll get the prayer chain started immediately. Hang in there. I'm sure the police will find her shortly. We have an outstanding force in Rocky Bluff."

"Thanks," Barb replied. "I'll let you know just as soon as we have any word on her whereabouts."

Barb hung up the phone, then dialed the Looking Glass. "Hello, Angie. You're on your own at the salon," she said, choking back the sobs that were beginning to overwhelm her. "Mother has wandered away in the snow. I've called the police to look for her. I'm afraid if they don't find her soon she'll freeze to death."

Angie's facial muscles tightened. "Don't worry about the salon; I'll take care of everything here. Let me know as soon as you find her."

Angie hung up the phone and walked to the window. *It's hard to imagine something this beautiful could possibly be deadly.*

CHAPTER 11

Jay Harkness sat at his desk in the Enlisted Men's Dormitory at Andersen Air Force Base, Guam. A picture of Angie Quinata was on the left, and his planning calendar was on the right. June fifteenth seemed so far away. He opened the worn envelope with the familiar postmark, Rocky Bluff, Montana, and reread the words. By now he could quote the letter line by line, but it was more comforting to see it on paper.

Dear Jay,
I'm sorry I haven't written for awhile. Taking classes while I'm working part-time is consuming all my time. I was back in Rocky Bluff this past weekend and learned that John Paterson will be leaving his position as Computer Systems manager at Rocky Bluff Community College. He's going to be attending the university for advanced training

this fall and wanted to train his replacement over the summer.

Also, this past summer there was a change of administration at the college. President Oaks retired, and our high school principal, Grady Walker, was selected in his place.

If you're interested in the position, I'm sure he'll look favorably on his old basketball star.

Keep in touch,
Ryan

This is too good to be true, Jay told himself. *I thought I'd have to go to one of the larger cities in Montana to get a job in computers. I can hardly wait to let Angie know.* Jay sat at his desk in silence for a few minutes. *Maybe I better write to the college and apply for the job before I tell anyone. I don't want to have everyone disappointed if I don't get it.*

The remainder of the evening, Jay wrote and rewrote his resume. This was the first time he had applied for a job in his life. When he was a teenager, he worked after school, weekends, and summers at the family hardware store. After joining the military, his life had been dictated to him. After nearly three years, civilian life was looking more and more appealing, but he was finding he would have to take the initiative in job hunting himself. No one would do it for him.

Finishing his resume, Jay reached for the phone and dialed Angie's mother.

"Hello," Mitzi greeted.

"Hello, Mitzi. This is Jay. How are you doing?"

"I'm doing fine, except I miss that child of mine."

"I know. I didn't know it would be so lonesome without her. I can hardly wait to get there in June."

"Jay, I'm glad you called. I was just getting ready to call you," Mitzi Quinata said. "There are some airfare wars going on, and I was able to get a fairly inexpensive ticket to Great Falls for Christmas."

"How exciting. I wish I were going with you."

"While I'm there, I'm going to try to talk Angie into coming home with me. She sounds likes she's gotten over the shock of the attack so there's no reason for her to stay in Montana."

"She does appear to be healing emotionally," Jay agreed, "but I also get the feeling that she's falling in love with Rocky Bluff."

Mitzi ignored what Jay had said and immediately changed the subject to Angie's reactions to some of the uniqueness of Montana, especially the rodeos. It was good to talk with someone who also knew and loved Angie. They both chuckled and bade each other farewell.

A frown crossed Jay's face as he hung up the phone. He realized that Angie would again be faced with another decision between cultures, lifestyles, and romance.

Capt. Philip Mooney and Sgt. Scott Packwood took separate patrol cars and began systematically cruising the streets and alleys of Rocky Bluff looking for Maude Old Tail. After two hours they had covered all the streets in Rocky Bluff and returned to Barb's home.

With long faces they rang her doorbell. "Did you find her?" Barb asked anxiously.

"I covered all the streets and alleys east of here, and Scott cruised the streets and alleys to the west, but to no avail," Phil explained. "Is there any place she might have stopped to get warm?"

"The only places she's been to in Rocky Bluff is Dr. Brewer's office, the grocery store, and the church," Barb replied anxiously. "I'm sure they would have let me know if she turned up at any of them."

"Scott and I will check with businesses

downtown and see if anyone has seen her. If he takes everything north of Main Street and I take the businesses on the south, we can probably check them all in an hour," Phil said. "The important thing is that we find her before dark."

While Barb waited and prayed, her phone kept ringing with calls from concerned friends. Remembering how terrifying it was for Beth to be alone when her four year old was missing, Rebecca drove to Barb's home. "Barb, do you have anyone staying with you while you wait for word about your mother? I know minutes can seem like hours," Rebecca said as Barb greeted her at the door.

Tears filled Barb's eyes as Rebecca wrapped her arms around her friend. "Thank you for coming. I'm losing my mind with worry."

"Edith has the prayer chain working so I'm sure we'll get some good news soon," Rebecca said as the two women walked into the living room.

Barb had just poured Rebecca a cup of coffee when the phone rang for the twentieth time that afternoon. "Rebecca, would you mind answering that? I don't think I can answer any more questions."

"I'd be glad to," Rebecca said as she

reached for the phone. "Hello."

"Hello, Barb?"

"No, this is Rebecca Hatfield. May I help you?"

"Hi, Rebecca, this is Coach Watson. Has Mrs. Old Tail been found yet?"

"I'm afraid not. It's been nearly six hours now."

"We're getting ready to begin basketball practice, and everyday the team has to run at least two miles before we work on drills. I thought we could send the entire team out to run in different directions to look for Mrs. Old Tail."

"Todd, how ingenious. That's a great idea. I'll be sure and tell Barb."

Two cups of coffee later, there was still no word as to the whereabouts of Mrs. Old Tail. Phil Mooney and Scott Packwood returned with another unsuccessful report. All anyone could do was wait and pray.

Rebecca and Barb dozed all night and would awaken only to pace back and forth. At the first ray of sunlight, Barb made another pot of coffee and fixed toast for herself and Rebecca. Promptly at eight o'clock the doorbell rang. Fearing the worst, Barbara ran to the front door. She felt her heart drop to her feet as she saw Pastor Rhodes through the peephole. She solemnly opened the door.

"Mother!" Barb shouted as she embraced her aging parent. "Are you all right?"

"I'm fine," Maude Old Tail's eyes were blank and unresponsive. "What's for breakfast? I'm hungry."

"Pastor Rhodes, where did you find her?" Barb asked as tears of joy flowed unashamedly down her cheeks.

"I was going into the sanctuary of the church early this morning to change the banner before the Sunday service and found her sleeping in a pew. Someone must have inadvertently left the side door unlocked."

"Thank God for that," Barb gasped. "Her guardian angel must have really been looking out for her. It's amazing how God uses someone's mistake to save someone else's life. Thank you so much for bringing her home."

Pastor Rhodes smiled as he turned to leave. "It was my pleasure. I'm thankful everything turned out well for everyone."

Rebecca fixed a large breakfast of bacon, eggs, toast, and juice while Barb helped her mother bathe and dress. She relished the task since a few hours before she thought she would never have the opportunity of showing her love to her mother again. While her mother ate, Barb dialed Edith Dutton's number.

"Edith, our prayers have been answered," Barb nearly shouted in the phone. "Pastor Rhodes found Mother sleeping in one of the pews in the church this morning."

"Thank the good Lord," Edith replied calmly. "I knew He wouldn't let us down. I'll let the others on the prayer chain know that their prayers were answered and your mother is safe."

"I know one thing," Barb stated matter-of-factly. "I'll never be able to leave Mother home alone again, but I don't know how I'll be able to even work part-time. I've never heard of adult day care services in Rocky Bluff."

"Until something opens up for you, why don't you bring your mother over here while you go to work?" Edith suggested. "I won't be able to do much except to fix a salad or sandwich for lunch, but I could give you a call if she becomes disoriented and insists on going outside."

"Edith, I can't ask you to do that. You've spent your entire life helping others," the concerned daughter replied.

"That's why I want to do it," the older woman protested. "I don't want to feel set on the shelf and passed over. I want to continue living life and helping others just as long as I can."

Barb and Edith continued making detailed plans, and Barb agreed to bring her mother the next morning at ten. By the time they finished their conversation, Rebecca had finished the morning dishes, and Mrs. Old Tail was comfortable in her favorite chair watching her favorite game show. Rebecca said good-bye to her friend, and Barb sank into the cushions of the sofa with exhaustion. Rocky Bluff had survived another crisis by pulling together and helping one another.

Nancy Harkness had prepared a large Thanksgiving dinner for her husband, Bob, her mother-in-law, Edith, and her daughter, Dawn. After nearly three months at Montana State University, Dawn had returned for the holidays just the day before. Dinner-table conversation centered around Dawn's college activities. Every time they asked about her social life, she changed the subject to her classes and midterm tests.

Sensing her discomfort about talking about her social life at college, Edith queried, "How are you going to spend your vacation in Rocky Bluff?"

"Tomorrow Tara and I plan to get up early and go skiing. With the early snowfall this year they say there's a good snowpack on the slopes."

Edith looked thoughtful for a moment. "Honey, would you do me a favor? Would you mind asking Angie to go with you? She keeps talking about wanting to learn to ski, but she doesn't know anyone who does."

Dawn rolled her eyes and took a deep breath. "I suppose we could give her a ride, but she'll have to stay on the bunny run until she learns how. We want to do some serious skiing. Maybe we could get the lodge's ski pro to give her lessons while we go to the slopes."

"Thanks, Dawn. I'll give you enough money for gas, everyone's ski lift tickets, and rental money for Angie's skis." Edith paused, then chuckled. "I wonder if Angie will be interested in skiing after her first trip to the slopes. I'll never forget how appalled she was after she went to the rodeo last summer."

At six o'clock the next morning, the three young women headed toward the ski lodge in Dawn's minisized car. Angie marveled at the picturesque beauty of the snow lacing the pine trees. The magnificence of the rising sun reflected across glistening snow. Her dream of learning to snow ski was finally coming true.

Arriving at the ski lodge, Dawn immediately found the ski pro. "Duke, we brought a friend along who's fresh off the boat from Guam. She's really anxious to learn to ski so she'll have something to write home about. Will you have time to give her lessons today?"

Duke surveyed the petite dark-haired woman standing with Tara Wolf. "Just leave her to me," he chuckled. "She'll be in good hands."

"Thanks; you're a dear," Dawn replied and hurried out the door. Approaching her friends, Dawn shouted, "Angie, you're in luck. The ski pro said he'd stay with you until you can ski on your own. Tara, let's hit the slopes."

Angie watched her two companions hurry toward the ski lift as advanced skiers whisked down the slopes. *Why did I even come? What makes me think I can learn to do that? I would probably break my leg the first trip down.*

"Hello. You must be Angie," a deep voice behind her said.

She whirled. A tall, thin, bearded man smiled down at her. "Yes, and you must be the ski instructor."

"Duke Harrington in person. In a few short hours I'll have you whisking down those slopes with the best of them."

Angie shuddered as a fresh blast of cold air hit her cheeks. "I'm a pretty slow learner."

"First things first, let's go inside and fit you with skis," Duke directed as he put his hand on her shoulder. "What size shoes do you wear?"

"Five and a half," Angie responded as she felt her freezing cheeks blush.

The next half hour the ski instructor explained the variations in skis and the type of bindings she'd need. He then took her outside where he helped her put on her skis, then slipped into his own. He demonstrated how to push off, stop, and steer to the right and left. Angie clumsily copied his movements.

"Let's have some hot chocolate before we hit the bunny run," he said as he motioned to the small coffee shop at the corner of the lodge. "I'll be right with you. I need to check in with my office."

"Sure," Angie replied as she headed for the lodge. "I could use a break."

As Angie sipped her hot chocolate, she watched Duke's tall physique in the distance. Even with heavy clothing she could see his firm muscles bulging under his coat. The beard was a novelty. Only on TV and in the movies had she seen beards. *That beard is so distinguishing. It's just too hot to wear them on Guam. I wonder how his wife likes it?* Angie silently giggled. *I wonder how much trouble he has eating?*

Duke returned to Angie's table. "Can I order you a bowl of chili?"

"I'd love it," Angie replied and then blushed. "This is my first winter on the mainland so I've never had chili before."

"Try it; you'll like it."

After Duke placed their order, he told how during the summer he was a forest-fire fighter and when snow began to fly, he returned to being a skiing instructor. Angie was fascinated with his rugged lifestyle, so different from what she had grown up with. *It's interesting that Montana could turn out sophisticated, well-groomed men like Jay Harkness along with rugged, outdoorsmen like Duke Harrington. No wonder they say that Montana is a land of contrasts.*

The remainder of the afternoon, Angie spent conquering the bunny slope. Occasionally she would wave when she saw Dawn and Tara skiing down the advanced slopes. Duke was never far away . . . always cheering her on. Guam seemed a long way away. The crispness of the air rejuvenated her troubled spirit and relaxed her tense nerves.

At four o'clock Dawn and Tara skied to the base of the bunny slope. "Having fun, Angie?" Dawn asked as she began unbuckling her boots.

"This is great," Angie replied, her face aglow from exhilaration.

"I hate to call it quits, but it's going to be getting dark before long," Dawn apologized.

Angie looked over at her ski instructor. "I've got to come back and do this next weekend. I don't want to forget everything I've learned today."

"For someone who's never been around snow before, you learn faster than most of the natives. You'll be ready for the intermediate slopes by then," Duke replied. "I'll be waiting to see you next Saturday."

Angie took off her rented skis and handed them to Duke, while Dawn and Tara removed their skis and hooked them on top of the car. Duke put his arm around Angie. "I'll see you next Saturday," he whispered.

As the trio drove away from the ski lodge, Tara looked over her shoulder at Angie. "Duke sure is interested in you. Not every student gets that kind of personal attention."

"He won't spend that kind of time with

me next week," Angie protested. "Duke was just trying to get me off to a good start."

"Angie, don't be so naive," Dawn teased. "Duke was definitely trying to make time with you."

Angie's face flushed. *What if Dawn writes to Jay and tells him that someone else is interested in me? I'm sure everyone's going to be talking about Duke and me when nothing happened. He merely taught me to ski.*

Neither Rebecca nor Andy were home when Angie returned. The warmth of the house relaxed her. She went to the kitchen and fixed herself a cup of hot chocolate and found a couple of chocolate chip cookies to go with it. She sat at the kitchen table to enjoy her treat. There on the table was a letter in her mother's familiar handwriting. She hurriedly tore it open.

Dear Angie,
I took advantage of the recent price wars and bought a round-trip plane ticket to Great Falls. I'll be arriving December 15th and leaving January 5th. I can hardly wait to see you and have you show me Rocky Bluff.

I have some good news for you. Another beauty salon called the Hair Corner has taken over the space of Coiffure and Manicure. In just two months they have already built a good reputation. Yesterday I took the liberty of talking with the owner, and she was interested in you coming back and working for them.

I was so excited I could hardly stand it. I went directly to the travel agent. Since this was the last day of the cheap airfares, I purchased you a one-way ticket home. Things are working out too good to be true. I'm looking forward to your return. If you'd like to have your old room back, I'd love to have you, but if you'd rather have your own apartment, I'll try to find one for you.

I'm looking forward to seeing you the 15th.

Love,
Mom

Angie read and reread the letter. *I don't know if I want to go back to Guam. I can't leave Barbara now when she needs me the most. If I went back to Guam, I'd never be able to perfect my skiing skills. I wonder what Jay will want me to do?*

CHAPTER 12

Andy, Rebecca, and Angie dined leisurely in the Great Falls International Airport cafeteria. They made sure they were at the airport long before Mitzi's plane was due to arrive. They did not want Mitzi to repeat Angie's experience, alone in a strange land with no one to meet her.

Angie folded, unfolded, and refolded her napkin nervously. "Rebecca, what will I tell Mother? She bought a return airline ticket for me, but I don't want to use it. I'm not ready to return to Guam. But I don't want to hurt her feelings."

"Angie, if you don't want to return to Guam now, tell your mother that. Of course she'll be disappointed, but she'll understand."

"Maybe when she meets Edith, Nancy, Bob, and all my other friends in Rocky Bluff, she'll understand why I feel the way I do," Angie replied.

"Take her skiing, and maybe she'll love it so much, she'll decide to stay here," Andy teased.

"I'll admit skiing has become my life. Ever since Dawn first took me, I've been skiing every weekend," Angie laughed, then became serious. "But there's something more involved here than skiing. I made a commitment to Barb. She needs my help, and I'm beginning to build up a clientele."

"And your clientele is extremely well pleased with your work," Rebecca replied. Rebecca thought for a moment before she spoke again, and she tried to pick her words carefully. "Angie, before you make your decision, think about where you would be in five years if you went back to Guam. . . . And, if you decide to stay in Rocky Bluff, where would you be?"

"I love Rocky Bluff, and I'm looking forward to seeing Jay again," Angie replied. "I really miss him, but if I leave my job and go back to Guam now, the chances of us developing a permanent relationship when he gets out of the service will be slim or none."

"Explain that to your mother," Rebecca urged. "I'm sure she'll understand."

"She'll be heartbroken. I'm an only child, and she has centered her entire life around me. It's been hard for her to let me grow up."

"After she sees what you've accomplished in Rocky Bluff, she'll accept the fact that you're an adult now."

Andy glanced at his watch and reminded the others of the time. He paid the bill, and the trio hurried to the gate where Mitzi would deplane.

Angie eagerly scanned the passengers as they emerged from the ramp. She began to wonder if her mother had missed connections. When she finally spotted her weary mother, she was shocked how much grayer her mother's hair had become in the four months since she had last seen her. Angie ran into her mother's arms and cried unashamedly.

"Mom, how are you? I've missed you so."

"I've missed you too. Guam just hasn't been the same since you left."

Angie ignored her comment and stepped aside so Rebecca and Andy could greet her. Rebecca handed Mitzi one of her winter coats. "What's this?" Mitzi queried.

"You'll need this as soon as you step outdoors. It's five degrees below zero today."

"That's hard to believe," Mitzi replied as her eyes widened. "You mean you came out in that kind of weather? I'd think no one would leave their homes with temperatures like that."

"This is nothing," Andy chuckled. "Montanans only stay indoors during major blizzards, and those only happen every few years. We're prepared to live with snow and cold, so nothing slows us down."

Angie took her mother's arm, and they walked toward the baggage claim. She would tell her mother of her decision later, but right now she wanted to bask in the pleasure of her presence.

During the return trip to Rocky Bluff, Mitzi's eyes sparkled as she scrutinized the banks of snow beside the highway. She eagerly shared some of her adventures in flying, but gradually jet lag began to overtake her. She leaned her head on the back of the seat and fell asleep. Angie smiled with amused understanding. *I felt exactly the same way when I arrived. Everyone wanted to talk, and all I wanted to do was sleep.*

Arriving at the Hatfields' home, Mitzi went right to bed and slept for twelve hours straight. Everyone tiptoed around the house in order not to awaken her. Finally, Mitzi emerged from her bedroom rested and eager to see Rocky Bluff. Rebecca suggested their first stop should be the Burr and Saddle Cafe. Its Western motif and Montana hospitality projected the true spirit of relaxed Rocky Bluff.

Mitzi glanced through the menu. "Almost everything here is beef."

"Enjoy it," Rebecca laughed. "You're in cattle country now."

"I guess I'm used to a diet of pork, seafood, and rice, but this won't be hard at all to get used to."

While they were eating, Duke Harrington entered the cafe, spotted Angie, and walked straight to her table. "How's my favorite skiing student?" he chuckled.

"I'm fine," Angie replied as she turned to the others. "I'd like you to meet my mother, Mitzi Quinata, and my Rocky Bluff hostess, Rebecca Hatfield. This is Duke Harrington."

"How do you do?" Duke said with overdone politeness. "Mrs. Quinata, you have a lovely daughter."

Mitzi glanced at Angie's flushed face, then back to Duke. "Thank you. I couldn't agree with you more."

Duke then turned to Rebecca. "Would you be any relation to Andy Hatfield?"

"Yes. He's my husband. Do you know him?"

"Every year he teaches classes in firefighting to our new recruits in the forest service. He's quite a guy."

Mitzi's eyes widened. "You mean you fight forest fires besides giving ski lessons?"

"In summer I fight forest fires and in winter I work at the ski lodge, so I'm never unemployed."

"How exciting," Mitzi gasped.

Duke turned to leave. "It's nice meeting you folks. I hope you'll be coming to the mountain soon. The ski lessons will be on me."

As Duke joined a friend in the far booth, Mitzi turned to her daughter. "He's a very nice young man. I think he really likes you."

"I'm just another one of his many ski students," Angie protested.

"For such a polite man, he looks awfully shaggy with hair all over his face," Mitzi noted.

"He says it keeps him warm up on the ski lift."

"I guess that makes sense," Mitzi said as she turned back to her Salisbury steak. She silently chuckled as the local men entered the restaurant wearing cowboy hats and boots. *This is even better than the old-fashioned Westerns on TV,* she told herself.

Angie enjoyed the company of her mother after a separation of nearly six months, but a wall remained between them, and the conversation was superficial. *How will I ever tell her I'm not returning to Guam with her? Will she be so upset with me that we can't enjoy our time together? Should I wait for her to bring up the subject, or should I?*

During the entire lunch, Mitzi studied her daughter and listened to her trivial chatter. *Has Angie changed? She used to be open and honest with me and often ridiculed idle chatter. Has six months made this much difference?*

After finishing lunch, Rebecca drove the Quinatas to the Looking Glass Salon. Angie proudly showed her workplace to her mother and introduced her to Barb Old Tail. "Mrs. Quinata, it's so nice to meet you. I can't tell you how happy I am to have Angie with me. She's an answer to my prayers. I don't know what I'd do without her. I'm afraid I'd either have to put my mother in a nursing home or quit work all together."

Mitzi gulped. *What will poor Barb do when Angie returns to Guam?* she pondered. "I'm glad Angie could help you. She's always dreamed of becoming a beautician."

"She's been a real jewel," Barb replied as her next customer walked into the salon.

Rebecca glanced at her watch and turned to Mitzi. "I told Edith Dutton, Jay's grandmother, that we'd stop by for coffee this afternoon. Jay's mother is also going to be there putting up Christmas decorations."

"I'm anxious to meet them," Mitzi smiled. "I heard so much about them. Jay has presented them as super women."

"They are extra special people, just like Jay has said," Angie said as they walked through the snow toward Rebecca's car.

A half hour later, Rebecca, Mitzi, and Angie made themselves comfortable in Edith Dutton's living room. Mitzi admired the string of lights Nancy Harkness had hung around the window. She had decorated the tree in the corner with white lights and red bows. Mitzi was more than happy to relate as many anecdotes about Jay as she could remember. "I haven't told Jay yet, but I was able to get an inexpensive one-way ticket so Angie can return to Guam with me. There's even a salon interested in hiring her when she gets back."

Edith examined the young woman sitting nervously across the room. "Angie, you didn't tell us you were leaving so soon."

Angie looked at her mother, then at the floor. "I'm not. I love it here, and I don't want to hurt Mother, but I can't return now. Barb needs me. Besides I want to be here when Jay gets out of the service this summer."

Tears filled Mitzi's eyes. "You mean I

wasted my money on that ticket? I thought for sure you'd want to come home. Every Guamanian who leaves the island gets homesick and returns within a few months. I thought you loved Guam and your family. You have aunts, uncles, and cousins in nearly every village."

Angie joined her mother in tears. "Mother, I do love you and all of my other relatives there, but I just can't return now. I hoped you'd understand. For once in my life I have to do what I think is right, whether anyone agrees with me or not."

"I love you and have missed you so much since you went away," Mitzi sobbed. "I suppose I should have asked you before I bought that ticket. I just wanted to surprise you. I didn't realize that you'd begun an entirely new life here. I was foolish to have wasted my money."

Rebecca, Edith, and Nancy watched the mother-daughter encounter with deep compassion and understanding. Both Edith and Nancy had experienced the struggles of letting their own children grow up. Nancy especially remembered the pain she and Bob had known when Jay decided to enlist in the Air Force rather than go to college.

"Maybe it's not all wasted," Nancy said. "I haven't told anyone, but I've been setting money aside every month so I could go to Guam and see Jay before he comes home. I could buy your ticket to Guam, then buy the return ticket from a local travel agent."

Mitzi looked up and dried her eyes. "I don't want you to feel obligated. I should have checked with Angie first."

"I'm not doing this out of obligation. I'm doing this because I want to visit Jay while he's still on Guam," Nancy protested.

Mitzi broke into a broad grin. "If you'd be going anyway, that's a good idea. I know Jay will be anxious to see you. I'd love to have you stay with me while you're there. Who knows, someday we may be sharing grandchildren."

Angie flushed. "Please don't rush things. We're not even officially engaged yet."

As the days flew by, Angie and Mitzi enjoyed each other's company more than ever before. They had both learned to relate to each other as woman-to-woman. Angie loved showing her mother the community and introducing her to friends. While Angie was working, Mitzi spent time with Rebecca and Edith. She'd always known family togetherness on her island home, but never before had she felt such community togetherness as she did in Rocky Bluff. *If Angie stays here and marries Jay, maybe I'll retire to Montana instead of staying on Guam. It may be cold here, but the personal warmth of the people negates the weather.*

Early Saturday morning, Rebecca, Mitzi, and Angie headed for the ski slopes fifty miles north of town. Duke met them at the pro shop. "Hello. Are you ready to try your hand at skiing?"

Rebecca and Mitzi looked at each other. "I'm game if you are," Mitzi giggled. "If we both break our legs, Angie's here to drive us home."

Duke helped them select rental skis and boots. Angie picked out her favorite set and had them on within minutes. "I'll leave you two at the bunny slope for your lessons. I'm going to try to conquer the intermediate. If I'm successful, maybe I'll even take on the advanced slope today."

Mitzi wrinkled her forehead. "Are you sure you're up to the advanced slope? You've only been skiing less than a month."

"Normally I'd agree with you," Duke replied with pride, "but she's an amazingly fast learner."

Both Mitzi and Rebecca ended up face-down in the snow several times. Age had helped remove much of their self-consciousness. When they fell, both would lay in the snow and laugh at themselves, while Duke looked on with puzzlement. *This is really different trying to teach women over fifty to ski. They'll never learn if they don't quit laughing. They're worse than junior high school students.*

Angie joined them for a late lunch in the coffee shop. "Well, are you ready to hit the slopes again?"

"Every muscle in my body aches, and I'm cold to the bone," her mother moaned.

"Do you want to go home then?"

"Oh, no. Enjoy yourself. We'll just sit in the lodge and sip hot chocolate while we watch you conquer the slopes."

"Thanks, Mom. I'm so glad you came to Rocky Bluff. This is the best Christmas season ever."

Mitzi leaned over and hugged her daughter. "As soon as I get back, I'm going to start saving my pennies again so I can come back next Christmas. What better way to spend the holiday season than to feel the crispness of a snowy Montana breeze!"

On Christmas day Angie, Mitzi, and the Hatfields joined the entire Harkness clan at Nancy and Bob's home. How different it was from Angie's first meeting with the family soon after her arrival in Rocky Bluff. She had lost her shyness and self-consciousness.

In their own timing and their own way, each had learned of the tragedy which had befallen her on Guam. Angie was surprised that instead of being critical of her they loved her even more. Through them she had begun to come to accept the fact that she had been temporarily hurt, not damaged for life.

After the meal was over and the gifts opened, the family gathered in the living room to sing Christmas carols. In the midst of the merrymaking, the telephone rang, and Nancy raced to answer it.

"Merry Christmas, Mom," Jay greeted.

"Merry Christmas to you."

"I finally got through," Jay sighed. "All the international phone lines have been busy for the last two hours. I suppose everyone is there enjoying themselves."

"Everyone but you. We all miss you, especially today."

"I miss you too. I can hardly wait to see you all. The next six months will probably go by very slowly."

"There might be a chance you'll be able to see one of us before then," Nancy said, trying to hide her excitement.

Jay wrinkled his forehead in puzzlement. "Who's that?"

"Me. That is, if it doesn't conflict with

your work."

"I'll always have time to work in my mother," Jay laughed, "but what's up?"

"Did you know that as a Christmas present Mitzi bought a cheap, one-way ticket for Angie to return to Guam?"

"No! Is Angie coming back with her?"

"No, Barb Old Tail can't get along without her, and Angie loves her work and Rocky Bluff. Mitzi was just overeager. She thought she was doing Angie a favor."

Jay shook his head. "It's too bad she wasted her money without first checking with Angie."

"It's not totally wasted. I decided to buy the cheap ticket from her and then get a return ticket from the local travel agent. She even invited me to stay with her while I'm on the island."

Jay beamed. "Great! When are you going to come?"

"If the dates are suitable with you, I'll fly to Guam with Mitzi on January fifth and stay until the twentieth."

"I can hardly wait," Jay replied.

Nancy turned on the speakerphone and the entire family got in on the conversation with Jay. He was most interested in learning how business was going at the hardware store from his father and how the new satel-

222

lite store in Running Butte was doing from his aunt. They all wished each other a merry Christmas; then Nancy switched off the speakerphone so Angie could have a private conversation from the bedroom extension.

The young couple lovingly greeted each other, and each asked how the other was doing. Finally, Angie could no longer hold back the real issue on her mind. "Jay, I miss you and can hardly wait until we can be together, but I hope you understand why I made the decision to stay in Rocky Bluff."

"I'm glad you did. I'll be home in six months; then we'll spend the rest of our lives together."

Angie paused. *Before the attack those words would have been music to my ears. After the attack I would have said "no way," but now I'm not sure. I love Rocky Bluff and all Jay's relatives, but there's so much I want to experience before I settle down — improving my skiing, learning to ride horseback, sightseeing across the rest of the mainland.*

"I'm looking forward to seeing you again," Angie replied evasively. "We have had so much fun together."

Jay told her that he'd applied for the Computer Systems manager position at the local community college and how much he wanted that position. Angie told Jay about her new love for skiing, but she avoided any mention of Duke Harrington and her skiing lessons. She was sure Duke was merely a passing novelty in her life.

The remaining days of her mother's vacation flew by. A bond deeper than ever before built between them. Mitzi finally accepted the fact that Angie was now an adult and responsible for the decisions in her life, and Angie realized that her mother's overprotectiveness was motivated out of love. Saying good-bye was excruciatingly painful for both of them.

For three days after her mother's departure, Angie remained in a blue mood. To console herself, on Saturday Angie went to the ski slopes. The ski runs were nearly deserted when she arrived. As she was lacing her boots, Duke Harrington appeared. "Mind if I join you on the ski lift?" he greeted.

"Sure. Why not?"

On the way up the lift, Duke chattered about the condition of the snow and the warmth of the weather. Angie watched him with curiosity. Very rarely did he leave his post at the ski lodge before his replacement came.

When the pair arrived at the top, Duke motioned for her to follow him. His eyes gleamed with strange haughtiness. "Let's rest on this boulder before we go down," he suggested.

Angie crouched in the snow, while Duke leaned his back against the rock. "Tell me about your boyfriend back in Guam," he prodded. "I heard he was a local boy."

Angie wrinkled her forehead. "His name is Jay Harkness. His folks run the Harkness Hardware Store in Rocky Bluff."

"I remember him. He was a couple of years ahead of me in school. He was known as a real jock back then," Duke sneered.

"He did tell me that he loved sports and participated in almost all of them," she replied, trying to lighten up the situation. "They said he couldn't try out for girls' basketball," she giggled.

"You've been here a long time without him," Duke said as he scooted in the snow until he was beside her. "I bet you miss a little loving." With that he took Angie in his arms and planted a heavy kiss on her lips. She drew back, instinctively slapped his face, sprang to her feet, and raced down the ski run. Her legs trembled as she approached the lodge. Flashbacks to six months before enveloped her. Quickly unlacing her boots and abandoning the rental skis at the door of the pro shop, Angie jumped into Rebecca's Chrysler and raced toward Rocky Bluff.

Several miles down the road, she began to relax. This was the second time a man had violated her. The first time she had felt guilt, humiliation, shame, and self-condemnation. This time she felt only anger. *If only everyone had the same concern and respect for the opposite sex as Jay has,* she thought. *I really appreciate all the love and advice I received from everyone in Rocky Bluff. As Edith reminded me so many times since I've been here, it's not the exciting men who make the best husbands; it's those who are as comfortable as an old pair of shoes.*

CHAPTER 13

Angie basked in the warm spring air as she walked the twelve blocks from the Looking Glass Beauty Salon to the Hatfields' home. Springtime in the Rockies was even more beautiful than Jay had described. She marveled at the return of the robins. Birds had disappeared from Guam many years before when the brown tree snake had taken over the island and devoured them. Tulips were blooming in the yards, and the lilac bushes were on the verge of bursting forth. Some of the neighbors were tilling up a section of their backyards for a garden. *When I get a home of my own, I want to try gardening. It looks so rewarding to watch your food grow from a seed instead of having everything shipped in cans and boxes.*

As Angie opened the front door, Rebecca hurried from the kitchen to greet her. "Angie, Jay just called. He was so disappointed that he'd missed you. He has something exciting to tell you. He'll call back at six o'clock our time."

"Did he give you any idea of what's happening?"

"Jay said it was something very exciting, and he wanted you to be the first one in Rocky Bluff to know."

Angie took off her sweater and hung it in the hall closet. "I can't imagine what it'd be. Jay is usually pretty laid-back and seldom gets excited."

For the next half hour Angie stayed close to the phone. She took a soft drink from the refrigerator and sat in an easy chair to read the *Rocky Bluff Herald.* Every few minutes she glanced at the clock over the TV. Promptly at six o'clock, the telephone rang. "Hello, Hatfield residence."

"Hello, Angie," Jay Harkness greeted. "How are you doing?"

"I'm curious. What's your good news?" Angie replied lightly.

"Remember me telling you about my high school principal, Grady Walker?"

"Yes."

"He's now the president of Rocky Bluff Community College, and he just offered me the job of Computer Systems manager at the college. The present manager leaves September first, but Mr. Walker wants me onboard in July. Isn't that great?"

"Jay, I'm so proud of you. I knew all your hard work at computer school would pay off."

"I'm just glad I can come back to Rocky Bluff. With my specialized training I expected that I'd have to go to one of the major cities to obtain a job."

"I couldn't imagine any town could be as friendly as you claimed, but it definitely lived up to your description," Angie replied. "I now understand why you're so eager to come home."

"Angie, I hate to hang up, but I need to call my folks and let them know before I go to work. I'll call you again next week."

Angie said good-bye and retreated to her basement room. She flopped across her bed and closed her eyes. *What would life be like with Jay back in Rocky Bluff?* She pictured herself running into his arms at the airport . . . dining out together . . . watching videos together . . . taking long walks together hand in hand . . . talking and laughing together. That was their life together in Guam, but this was Rocky Bluff.

Jay has always assumed our relationship would deepen when he returned, but am I ready for a more permanent relationship? If he should formally ask me to marry him, what should I say? How long should we be engaged before we marry? What if Jay doesn't like what I've become and wants to break off the friendship? Should I immediately return to Guam? I don't want to even consider that possibility.

Angie's anticipation grew with each passing day, causing her to become more and more restless. Her friends sympathized with her apprehension and tried to keep her occupied. Every weekend one of her Rocky Bluff friends took her on a minivacation to see the various sights of Montana: Yellowstone Park, Glacier Park, Virginia City, Helena, Fort Peck Reservoir, Flathead Lake. The vastness and beauty of the state overwhelmed her but could not mask her anticipation.

At long last, June fifteenth finally arrived. Angie made her third trip to the Great Falls International Airport, this time with Bob and Nancy Harkness. The miles seemed to never end as Angie's anticipation mounted. It had been ten months since she had last seen Jay. Fears began to overtake her. *Will he still love me after such a long separation? I treated him so rudely between the time of my assault and when I left the island. Will he have forgotten my cruel words? Will he have changed? Will he think I have changed into someone he's no longer comfortable with?* After several miles of worrying, Angie relaxed and conversed with the Harknesses in the front seat.

The miles faded away, and soon Bob was parking his car in the airport parking lot. They checked Jay's arrival gate on the monitor and hurried to the waiting area. Angie paced back and forth in the viewing area scanning the skies. Finally, she spotted a speck in the west which gradually became larger and larger.

Angie, Bob, and Nancy ran to the end of the loading ramp as the jetliner rolled to a stop. They scanned the deplaning passengers for a familiar face. Finally, a handsome, dark-haired passenger dressed in his best Air Force blues uniform appeared. Spotting his family, Jay broke into a run. He scooped Angie into his arms and swirled her around as tears ran down her cheeks. All of Angie's fears faded into oblivion. Jay had not changed. Jay embraced his mother, then his father. After being away for three years, Jay Harkness was finally back home in Montana.

"Would you like to stop for something to eat before we head back to Rocky Bluff?" Bob queried as they joined the others heading toward the baggage claim.

"Let's go to the Black Angus Steak House. The meat shipped to the base could not compare with good old Montana beef," Jay replied as he took Angie's hand. "The memory of the taste of a Montana filet mignon kept me going for three years."

Less than an hour later the Harkness family and Angie were gathered in a private booth in the Black Angus Steak House enjoying their steak dinners. "How's Dawn?" Jay asked his mother. "She hasn't written me for months."

Bob and Nancy exchanged nervous glances. "She says she's very busy with her sorority activities. She hasn't been home for several weeks."

"I've been concerned about her ever since I learned what sorority she joined. They have the reputation of being a wild bunch with a lot of drinking and partying. I know some of her friends' reputations," Jay replied, "and their reputations are not good."

"We're also very concerned," Nancy replied. "I hope that you'll be able to get through to her. We've tried, but she only shrugs it off and tells us we're not in tune with her generation."

Driving home, jet lag overtook Jay, and he slept most of the way. Angie sat silently beside him memorizing every curve and angle in his face. He was even more handsome than she had remembered. Once Jay was home, he went straight to bed and slept for two days.

After he was fully rested, he picked up the phone and called Angie at work. "Angie, can I pick you up after work and take you for a ride in the mountains? We can pick up some sandwiches and soft drinks to eat as we watch the sunset. We have a lot of catching up to do."

"I'd love it," Angie replied. "I'll be done by five tonight."

"Great. Grandma and Roy had their favorite spot in the mountains where they often went to watch the sunset. I'd like it to become our special place as well."

By six o'clock Jay and Angie were propped against a rock in the Big Snowy Mountains. "This is beautiful," Angie said as she held Jay's hand. "I can see why your grandparents liked it so well."

"Just to see the majesty of the mountains reflected in the lake has a way of putting one's troubles to rest. We have several more hours before the sun begins to set," Jay replied. "That's when words won't be able to describe the beauty."

"The long days are hard for me to get used to. In Montana there are only six and a half hours of darkness in the summer and only six and a half hours of daylight in the winter. On Guam there's hardly any variation in the length of the days."

Jay reached in his pocket and took out a small box and handed it to Angie.

"What's this?" she asked as she gingerly lifted off the lid, then burst out laughing. "Your friendship ring. I'm sorry that I gave it back to you the way I did that night in the hospital. That was so rude and unkind of me." Angie slipped the ring on her finger.

"I knew what you were going through when you returned it," Jay said as a mischievous twinkle appeared in his eye, "but I'm not going to give it back to you now."

Angie looked shocked. *Don't tell me that after I've waited so long for him to come home he's going to break up with me? Maybe I should have gone home with Mother at Christmas.* She handed the ring to Jay and muttered, "Why's that?"

"Because I have something better for you," Jay replied as he reached into the other pocket of his light jacket. He took out a small black velvet box. He opened the lid to show her the most beautiful marquee diamond she had ever seen.

"Angie, I love you so much and want you to wear this instead. Will you marry me? I promise to love and cherish you for the rest of my life."

Angie threw her arms around Jay. "Of course I'll marry you. We have been through so much together, and all the pain of it has drawn us closer together instead of separating us. I love you so, and I've been dreaming of this moment for months. But why did you have to tease me with the friendship ring?"

Jay's eyes again began to twinkle. "Just so you'd have a story to tell to our grandchildren. When I was little, I always bugged my grandparents about their romance, so I wanted to add a little color to our love story."

The cool mountain breeze refreshed the young lovers as they embraced. "Angie, we've been separated so long; I want to get married as soon as possible. Would the first part of September be too soon for you?"

"That sounds perfect," Angie replied. "I'll at least have a little time to plan a wedding."

"More important than the ceremony, I want to find a cozy bungalow of our own."

"Can we have a backyard big enough for a garden?" Angie queried.

"I'll even build a white picket fence if you'd like," Jay laughed.

Angie and Jay stayed at their special spot

until the last ray of sunlight was gone. There was so much to talk about and plan. Jay marveled at the confidence and self-reliance Angie had developed since she had come to Rocky Bluff. Their love was stronger than he could have ever imagined while he was waiting on Guam for this moment.

As they drove down the mountains in the darkness, Angie turned to her fiancé. "The first person I want to tell of our formal engagement is Mother. She's stuck with me through good times and bad."

"Let's call her as soon as we get to town. This is one call she's been waiting for since I gave you the friendship ring a couple of years ago. I'll even offer to buy half of her plane ticket if she will come to our wedding."

Mitzi was thrilled to get Jay and Angie's call. "Just let me know the date, and I'll be there," she nearly shouted into the phone. The next stop was Jay's parents. Angie proudly displayed the diamond ring and shared their tentative wedding plans. Half an hour later they were on their way to Edith Dutton's home. Jay's grandmother had been their strength through the tough times, and they were now overjoyed to share this happy time.

Two weeks later, Jay started his new job at

the college and spent many long hours learning the idiosyncrasies of their particular system. One evening while sitting in the Hatfields' backyard, he finally admitted his frustration. "Angie, I'd love to have a more active role in planning the wedding, but if you wait to talk every detail over with me, we'll never get anything done. Teresa Lennon used to plan a lot of weddings. I was at both the Reynolds' remarriage and the Blairs' wedding, and they were beautiful. Teresa masterminded both affairs."

"I'll talk to her," Angie replied. "She sure helped me get over my problems. I wonder why she's never remarried? At times she seems so lonely and tries to hide it by helping others."

Jay hesitated for a moment. "I've never thought about it that way," he replied, "but something traumatic must have happened to her a long time ago. She never talks about her past."

"That must be why she's so understanding about women's problems," she replied as she took another sip of her lemonade. "I'll give her a call tomorrow and see if she'll have time to help us."

Teresa was only too happy to plan for yet another wedding in Rocky Bluff. In the weeks that followed, she and Angie seemed to be everywhere — picking out a silverware pattern at The Bon, Angie's wedding dress and dresses for the bridesmaids at Fashion's by Rachel, and china and crystal at Laura's Jewelry Store. This wedding was fast becoming the social event of the year for Rocky Bluff.

CHAPTER 14

Amid her wedding preparations, Angie kept hearing the people of Rocky Bluff talk about how dry the weather was. Everyone began irrigating their lawns daily. She noted that the Hatfields' lawn was turning brown and asked Rebecca if she could water it.

"The mayor just ordered water rationing until further notice. Our city water supply is running dangerously low, and we need to have a reserve in case of a major fire," Rebecca replied. "There is to be no watering of lawns and washing of cars until further notice."

"That sounds serious," Angie gasped. "It's so different from Guam where they worry about typhoons with their torrential rainfalls."

"Andy is extremely concerned about the lack of water. He's been in close contact with the fire service in case a forest fire might break out in the area. The Fire

Management officer is afraid that if we don't get rain soon we'll burn."

Just as Andy and the Fire Management officer had anticipated, a lightning strike twenty miles from Rocky Bluff erupted into a fire about midnight that night. By morning the fire had already burned twenty acres. Firefighting crews were dispatched from all over the area. They immediately dug a fire line ten miles from Rocky Bluff, confident that it would contain the fire. However, two days later a hot southern wind fanned the flames across the fire line.

That morning, just five days before his wedding, Jay rushed into the Looking Glass Salon.

"Angie, the fire's jumped the fire line and is headed this way. They're calling for volunteers from the community to help dig firebreaks. They need every ablebodied person they can get so I volunteered. I hate being away from you just before our wedding, but if the town goes, there can be no wedding."

Angie's hand trembled. "I don't want anything to happen to you. Are you sure you won't be in danger?"

"I'll be far enough away from the actual fire, but the wind can be fickle, and you can never be too careful. Forest fires are one of the risks of living in Montana," he explained as he kissed her on the forehead and hurried out of the salon.

The fire was the talk of the town, and every client who came to the salon that day had an update from the fire line. Rumors abounded. As Angie walked home that evening, her eyes continually drifted to the red glow and black smoke in the northern skies. Somewhere out there her love might be in serious danger.

For three days Rocky Bluff seemed to be on hold as the fire spread. It jumped several secondary roads, and the main road north was closed to all traffic. Several mountain cabins were destroyed. Businesses closed as more and more people joined the fire crews. Barb closed the beauty shop as no one was interested in having their hair done at a time like this. Pastor Rhodes called for a community-wide prayer vigil. Rocky Bluff was in a fight for its sheer survival.

As soon as Jay got to the fire camp, they immediately assigned him to a crew of twenty and handed him the appropriate equipment for building a fire line. Meals were brought to the site, and Jay did not return to the fire camp until darkness had settled over the mountain. As he was preparing for a few short hours of sleep, the Fire Management officer called to him.

"Jay, I understand that you were recently discharged from the Air Force," he said briskly. The sweat was rolling down his forehead and soaking his green forest service shirt.

"That's right, Sir. I just got back a couple months ago after more than two years on Guam."

"Did the military give you any medical training?"

"Yes, everyone gets first aid training."

"Good. We're short of medics. First thing in the morning, would you report to the medical tent. You'd be of more value to us there than on the fire line."

"I'd be glad to," Jay replied.

Jay was asleep as soon as he hit his bedroll. He hadn't been that tired since basic training. For the next three days, he helped treat blisters, minor burns, and heat exhaustion. Two firefighters had to be emergency evacuated to the hospital in Rocky Bluff. Jay was so busy at the medical tent he barely noticed the airplanes from Missoula flying over and dropping fire retardant on the fire and the helicopters dumping buckets of water. But the fire crept ever closer to Rocky Bluff.

On the fourth day a firefighter was brought

in who had been hit by a falling tree. As Jay checked him for possible broken bones, the young man asked, "Aren't you Jay Harkness?"

"Yes, I am," he replied. "You look faintly familiar, but I can't remember your name."

"My name's Duke Harrington. I was three years behind you in high school, but I went to all the basketball games you played."

"That was a long time ago," Jay chuckled. "I just got back after serving in the Air Force in Guam."

"I know," Duke replied dryly. "I met the Guamanian girl you sent home ahead of you. She's a mighty fine catch."

Jay wrinkled his forehead and finished his examination. "Angie is the most loving, compassionate person I've ever met. We're supposed to be married on Saturday."

"That's if the church is still standing," Duke replied sarcastically.

Jay finished examining Duke and applied salve to his burns and assigned him to a cot to recuperate. His wounds were superficial, but his tongue cut deeply into Jay's spirit which longed to be with his beloved.

Andy Hatfield went from street to street with his portable speaker system. "Prepare to evacuate. Prepare to evacuate. The fire is within five miles from town. Prepare to evacuate."

Rebecca knew exactly what to do: load her valuables in the car, hose down the house, and build a firebreak around the house by getting rid of all brush and shrubbery from next to the house.

"But isn't there anything else we can do? We're supposed to be married in two days," Angie nearly sobbed.

"Take the garden hose and soak down the house, especially the roof. If the fire does come this way, hopefully it will be too wet to ignite.

"It's all in God's hands now," Rebecca said and began chopping down her favorite shrubs. "Only a strong gully washer will put out this inferno, and the weather forecast is for more hot and dry temperatures."

As the two women frantically prepared to evacuate, Jay sped into the drive. He jumped from the car sweating and covered with dirt. Angie was immediately in his arms. "You're safe. You're safe."

"Some of us were sent to town to help people evacuate."

"I guess our wedding is off," Angie sobbed. "People in Rocky Bluff will soon lose their homes and everything they own, and there's nothing we can do about it."

"All we can do is pray," Jay said as he wiped the tears from Angie cheeks.

Suddenly, a loud clap of thunder echoed through the valley. All eyes turned westward. There a small storm cloud was beginning to build.

"Please, God, let that cloud bring rain," echoed throughout the community. People kept preparing to evacuate with one eye on that growing cloud in the west.

"Angie, do you feel that?" Jay asked.

"Feel what?"

"The wind is beginning to shift. It will fan the flames away from Rocky Bluff."

As the three exhausted workers stood on the front lawn of the Hatfields' home, the heavens opened and torrential rains poured from the skies. Angie took Jay's hand as the late summer rain immersed them. Slowly the smoke in the north subsided.

Angie thanked God for that rain as she silently told herself, *Just as the rain is quenching that flaming inferno, the healing love of Rocky Bluff has quenched my scorching pain and restored my life so that I can love again. Saturday will be even more special than before. Not only will the people of Rocky Bluff celebrate our healing love, they will also celebrate the healing water that saved their beloved city.*

ABOUT THE AUTHOR

Ann Bell is a librarian by profession and lives in Iowa with her husband, Jim, who is her biggest supporter. Ann has worked as a librarian and teacher in Iowa, Oregon, Guam, and Montana. She has been honored in the top three picks of *Heartsong Presents* members' favorite authors. Her eight *Heartsong* books all center around a fictional town in Montana called Rocky Bluff. She has also written numerous articles for Christian magazines and a book titled *Proving Yourself: A Study of James.*